SPECIAL MESSAGE TO READERS

This book is published under the auspices of

THE ULVERSCROFT FOUNDATION

(registered charity No. 264873 UK)

Established in 1972 to provide funds for research, diagnosis and treatment of eye diseases. Examples of contributions made are: —

A Children's Assessment Unit at Moorfield's Hospital, London.

•

Twin operating theatres at the Western Ophthalmic Hospital, London.

•

A Chair of Ophthalmology at the Royal Australian College of Ophthalmologists.

•

The Ulverscroft Children's Eye Unit at the Great Ormond Street Hospital For Sick Children, London.

You can help further the work of the Foundation by making a donation or leaving a legacy. Every contribution, no matter how small, is received with gratitude. Please write for details to:

**THE ULVERSCROFT FOUNDATION,
The Green, Bradgate Road, Anstey,
Leicester LE7 7FU, England.
Telephone: (0116) 236 4325**

**In Australia write to:
THE ULVERSCROFT FOUNDATION,
c/o The Royal Australian College of
Ophthalmologists,
27, Commonwealth Street, Sydney,
N.S.W. 2010.**

NEMESIS RIDES THE TRAIL

Jo McQueen was raped and left for dead alongside the bodies of her parents, and thereafter she sought revenge on the three army deserters who had attacked her. She caught up with the first one in the middle of a stampede on a cattle drive. To catch number two, Jo enlisted the help of the notorious Mexican bandit, El Tigre. The third deserter was tracked down by Jo to a hideout in the hills, and a desperate shoot-out was to follow . . .

SAM FOSTER

NEMESIS RIDES THE TRAIL

Complete and Unabridged

LINFORD
Leicester

First published in Great Britain in 2001 by
Robert Hale Limited
London

First Linford Edition
published 2002
by arrangement with
Robert Hale Limited
London

The moral right of the author has been asserted

British Library CIP Data

Foster, Sam, *1920* –
   Nemesis rides the trail.—Large print ed.—
Linford western library
1. Western stories
2. Large type books
I. Title
823.9′14 [F]

ISBN 0–7089–9866–6

Published by
F. A. Thorpe (Publishing)
Anstey, Leicestershire

Set by Words & Graphics Ltd.
Anstey, Leicestershire
Printed and bound in Great Britain by
T. J. International Ltd., Padstow, Cornwall

This book is printed on acid-free paper

1

The New Hand

Chester squinted into the dawn light, making out the silhouettes of two riders approaching the chuck wagon. Nervously, he fingered the grey stubble on his jaw; visitors were rare on a trail drive.

'Mr Wade,' he called softly, and pointed.

The trail boss shaded his eyes and stared at the new arrivals; he eased his Colt in its holster and walked towards them.

Breakfast was over, the cowhands starting the herd north again after a night's rest. Chester had almost finished loading the wagon as he shared a last mug of coffee with the boss. He loaded the corral rope, standing close to a shotgun just behind the driver's seat.

He watched the meeting, straining

1

his ears for a clue to the intention of the riders. The first one dismounted and shook hands with Bill Wade; he heard a laugh, and relaxed. Could be old friends, he supposed, and watched the second rider astride a mule.

Words were exchanged but the morning breeze carried them away. His friend appeared to be urging the boss to do something, and Wade was reluctant.

The mule grazed, edging closer. Its rider seemed young and was dressed as a farmboy with a hunting rifle and a sheathed knife clipped to a waist-belt. As the light brightened, Chester saw the farmboy was a girl. Sixteen, perhaps, but big for her age.

He smiled, filled a mug with coffee and held it out. She slid from the saddle, took the mug and sipped, but said nothing. Her expression was sullen and her eyes blank; she stared back at him, without expression, above the rim of the mug.

Chester grew uneasy: was she one of those with something against ex-slaves with black skin? He recalled stories of zombies he'd heard in the deep South. If there was such a thing, this was how he imagined one might look.

Wade's friend rode off and the trail boss walked towards them, his face bleak.

'McQueen.' He addressed the girl. 'You'll ride with Chester on the chuck wagon. Make yourself useful and leave my cowhands alone.' He walked off towards his horse.

Chester looked at her, and wondered. Was she, perhaps, in the family way and were her parents unloading her on to some distant relative?

The sun rose higher. Chester finished loading the wagon and climbed into the driver's seat. 'You can hitch your mule behind,' he said softly.

She obeyed without a word and climbed up to sit beside him. Chester flicked his bull whip over the team's heads with a distinct crack, and the wagon lurched forward, following after the trail boss.

They led off in front of the herd. Two

thousand longhorns ambled behind, marshalled by cowhands, on their way from Texas to Kansas. The dust they raised could be seen for miles.

Chester thought: a silent one this, and kept quiet. As the sun climbed higher, the heat of day baked them. He glanced through the haze into the distance as he mentally planned the next meal. He pointed at her rifle.

'Can you use that thing, missy?'

He got a surly nod.

'You could be popular with the crew real quick if yuh shoot a deer for the pot. Saw some earlier over that way.' He indicated some low trees. 'You don't mind an old darkie speaking to yuh?'

She shook her head, swung down to the ground and unhitched her mule.

Chester said, 'Remember not to spook the cattle — shoot only when the wind's blowing away from us. If you start a stampede that'll not improve the boss's temper one bit.'

'I'm not stupid,' she said curtly, and rode off.

Chester smiled. It was the only effort she'd made at speech so far.

As McQueen turned her mule away from the herd, she ignored a friendly 'Hi!' from a cowhand she passed. Dust hung in a cloud over the land, and if Chester had really spotted deer, he still had keen eyesight.

It crossed her mind that he might just want to be rid of her. Or maybe Wade — Uncle Lew's so-called friend, who hadn't been exactly enthusiastic about welcoming her — had given orders to the negro cook. She wondered how much Uncle Lew had told the trail boss.

Beyond a flank rider she saw a small group of deer grazing, as if they'd never been hunted. Chester was right, she had to admit, and turned her mule slowly to get upwind.

She edged closer, testing the wind to make sure it hadn't changed. Her rifle was loaded and ready for action, as always. She had hunted for the pot many times . . . she dropped a mental shutter over that image. No longer was there a farm to return to, a family to hunt for; all that was buried in the past. Buried and best forgotten. The image persisted, frozen; her emotions froze with it. She would not allow tears.

Sight clearly, hand steady. Aim and squeeze, she told herself, the way she'd been taught.

A depressing thought came: it was hard to be an orphan at sixteen. Well, she'd find out soon enough if Uncle Lew really intended to help, or whether he was just putting her off. One thing at a time. Concentrate.

Her gaze fixed on a straggler, she sat easy in the saddle. One sweep around with her eyes. No cattle near and the wind blowing away from the herd. One shot was all that was needed.

She raised her rifle and sighted, and the lone deer became a man with red hair; his face changed; and changed again. One man, three faces.

She held her breath and squeezed the trigger. The man with red hair dropped and, as she rode closer, became the body of a deer.

The other deer scattered with graceful leaps, and she dismounted and butchered her kill. She cut the throat to let the blood drain and hacked out the best parts, packed them in a canvas sack and started back on the mule.

Nothing seemed to have changed. The prairie extended through a heat haze to a blurred horizon. The herd travelled slowly beneath a veil of dust. Drag riders urged on straggling longhorns. The faded blue of the sky was almost white, and the sun scorched.

Chester watched her face as she rode up to the chuck wagon; something had happened while she was away, but he wasn't sure what.

Her expression didn't have the same dead look as before, and he didn't like the change. Maybe she had acquired a taste for killing?

Chester kept his mouth shut and his eyes on the trail boss. Earlier than usual, Wade signalled a stop. The sun was still in the sky but they'd reached water. Chester turned his team towards a stand of trees and parked.

'If you will, missy, dry wood for a fire.'

She climbed down and began to collect twigs and small branches. Chester kept his matches carefully wrapped in wax paper, and soon had a fire going. She fed the fire while he set up his pots and pans, and chopped fresh meat for a stew.

Dust settled over everything as the cattle reached the river bank and cowhands drifted in.

'Smells good, Chester,' a puncher drawled.

'Give your thanks to McQueen.'

More men gathered, keeping their distance, until Chester shouted, 'Come and get it!'

There was a rush, men holding out metal plates as Chester dished up his stew. McQueen continued to feed the fire, where coffee was boiling.

She was careful about keeping to

herself, he noted, ignoring the joshing cowhands. She said nothing and ate little. Strange in one so young living outdoors.

'Better eat something, missy. You'll need to keep up your strength.'

Then Pike rode in. Chester had been waiting to see her reaction to the outfit's acknowledged Romeo. Dark-haired with a ready grin, obviously he'd have to try to charm the new hand.

The young cowboy ambled over to the fire, apparently confident of an easy conquest. He looked her up and down, appreciating her well-filled shirt and tight jeans. It was an insolent stare, and his voice was an impudent drawl.

'Reckon you and me will get together this drive, Queenie.'

McQueen reacted swiftly and violently. She straightened immediately, turning to face him. 'Quit looking at me like I was one of your cows or I'll take your eyes out!'

She took one step forward and her knife came from its sheath like a flash of metal lightning, still stained with the deer's blood. She slashed at Pike's face and Chester didn't doubt she meant what she said. Neither did anyone else around the chuck wagon.

Pike would have been scarred for life if he hadn't stepped backwards in a hurry, his face pale with alarm. The high heel of his cowboy boot caught in a tuft of grass, and he stumbled and fell flat on his back. It was only the fall that saved him.

'Crazy woman,' he muttered, making no effort to get up. Other cowhands edged away; only Bill Wade moved to intervene, angrily.

Chester reached for his bull whip; a quick flick and the lash snaked out, curled around McQueen's blade and neatly lifted the knife from her hand.

She turned on him. 'Mind your own damned business, Chester!'

Wade snapped, 'Back off, Pike. You're out of order. Try anything like that again, and I'll sack yuh on the spot. Or any other man.'

He glared at her. 'And you, McQueen. Threaten one of my men again and I'll dump yuh, no matter who your uncle is. Now get in the chuck wagon and stay there — tomorrow, you'll ride drag.'

Pike got to his feet and laughed. 'Eat my dust, Queenie!'

She took her knife from Chester, sheathed it and climbed silently into the wagon. The cowhands looked the other way.

Chester exchanged a glance with Bill Wade. The trail boss had a grim expression. Was that why his friend had insisted she travel north with the drive? Had she killed someone and was fleeing the law?

2

Men with Red Hair

It was a nightmare, the usual one, but she couldn't stop it recurring. She was often scared to go to sleep at night. Sometimes she tried to stay awake, but failed, and relived that day again and again.

The dream was a jumble, a mishmash of pain and blood and gunshots. It was not something she wanted to relive, but it was forced on her, like the rape . . .

* * *

Three men had ridden up to the homestead; one dressed all in black and carrying a Bible, one dressed as a cowhand, and one still partly in army uniform on a big black stallion. The thing that made them stand out in her memory was that each man had red hair.

Her father had welcomed them, as he would any visitor to their lonely homestead. It was a chance for news in exchange for a meal.

The one addressed as Preacher spoke in solemn tones: 'God is my strength and power; and he maketh my way perfect. Strangers shall submit themselves to me; as soon as they hear my voice, they shall be obedient to me.'

'Especially women,' grunted the one called Solo.

Her father became angry, and the Bible changed into a gun that fired and fired again, and her father was falling and her mother screaming and the nightmare began.

The Preacher intoned, 'Thank you, Lord, for delivering me from a man of violence.'

She saw her father's body jerk like a puppet on strings as each bullet struck home. He was trying to say something but only small gasps came out. Her mother was on her knees, crying over him when the third redhead — the one in army tunic known as Fletch — used his boot to kick her away.

She saw no more because a bony fist crashed into her face, mashing her lips against her teeth. Bright pain brought tears to her eyes and blood spurted from her nose. She fell back against a plank wall and slid to the floor, dazed, struggling to breathe through her mouth.

She heard again the agony in her mother's voice, 'No, not Jo, me . . .'

The cowboy, Solo, mocked, 'Guess these fillies need some discipline,' and removed his belt. 'We give the orders now. The young one first.'

She remembered bristly faces, exhaling a smell of whiskey, looming above her, one after another; she'd never forget those faces, never. She lay like a log, half-stunned and frozen inside, shuddering under their hands.

The last one hit her again, and she

blanked out. When she came to, there were the remains of a meal on the table and they were playing cards and drinking.

Her mother was crawling across the floor towards her. The three red-haired men in her nightmare grinned and, as if it were no more than a casual after-thought, one drew his Colt and shot her mother.

'The Lord giveth, and the Lord taketh away!'

Jo lay as if paralysed. She knew there was no help within miles; she was bruised, her body ached and she wept blood. She was bewildered and frightened as the Preacher lifted his voice in anger.

'Enough fornicating — finish her off, Fletch. Solo, get the horses, and be careful of that black brute. It's time to move on before someone comes visiting.'

He ransacked the house for what food, drink and money was left and walked outside.

'Kill,' muttered the one in the army tunic, lurching towards her with a fire-iron. He struck at her, but was too drunk to aim his blow and the iron barely grazed her. He dropped it and staggered outside.

She heard hoofbeats fading in the distance, and there was a long, unreal silence, then sobbing. After a while she realized she was making the sound and stopped. She lived with their names — one, two, three; Preacher, Solo, Fletch — engraved on her brain and hate pulsing through her like a drum-beat, demanding revenge . . .

She screamed herself awake, soaking in sweat, and a soft voice crooned, 'Quiet now, missy. If you scare them steers the way you scared me, they won't stop running this side of Canada.'

Gradually she became aware of her bedroll tangled up beneath the chuck wagon, the prairie endlessly stretching away, starlight in a night sky, Chester's voice.

He crooned a lullaby, keeping his distance, careful not to touch her.

She struggled alert, gulping air into her lungs, calming herself. The day of the nightmare was in the past, and the time for revenge had yet to arrive.

Chester held out a water bottle. 'Throat must be plumb wore out, I'd say.'

She took it gratefully, conscious of a dull ache at the back of her throat, pulled the plug, rinsed out her mouth and spat. She forced herself to drink slowly, counting swallows, till she regained control.

She replaced the plug and handed the bottle back. 'Thanks.'

Chester smiled in the dark, white teeth gleaming, and she wondered how much she'd revealed in her nightmare. Apparently he had the ability to read her face.

'Ain't nothin' I ain't heard a hundred times before, missy.'

He removed his shirt and turned so she could see the criss-crossing weals on his back.

'An awful lot of people get hurt in this life, missy. You're not alone. My wife, my daughters too — female slaves have their uses. Always enough trash to go around.' He sighed and put his shirt back on.

'Yes, trash,' she agreed. 'Chester, will you teach me to use a bull whip the way you handle it?'

'I can try. Takes a knack, and an eye.' He rose slowly. 'Getting light already so I'll start a fire to cook breakfast. You take it easy, 'cause the boss wants you on drag, remember.'

She dozed, rose late and splashed water from a barrel on the wagon over her face, and made a hurried breakfast. The horse wrangler brought in his remuda of cowponies and the riders saddled up.

Wade said, 'McQueen, leave your mule with Chester. Cowponies know about cattle. Get behind the herd with the other drag riders and make sure any stragglers keep up.'

'Sure, boss,' she said meekly.

The other men left her strictly alone after the way she'd gone for Pike. She noticed the would-be Romeo keeping his distance as he saddled his mount.

The herd started slowly, reluctant to leave water, and gradually became strung out. She followed the other drag riders to get behind the last few steers. Dust rose in a choking cloud, and she copied the men when they put up their bandannas to cover their mouth and nostrils.

Wade was clever; drag riders were needed, so the job was handy as a goad to keep anyone awkward in line.

The trail boss let the animals set the pace; hurrying took off pounds of meat and reduced their price at the railhead.

He was right, too, about her pony; she need only sit easily in the saddle, and let it head off the cows who were inclined to wander.

She saw another drag rider pull his gun to shoot a calf and then use the end of his lariat to urge the mother to rejoin the herd. McQueen had grown up on a farm and wasn't sentimental about animals; to have let the calf slow them down was not an option on a trail drive.

She rode alone, herding stragglers as necessary, remembering her nightmare and what followed: homesteaders coming by and stopping to help; the ride into town on their wagon, held by an elderly woman; the doctor fussing around her; and, finally, the telegraph message to Uncle Lew . . .

Uncle Lew, in town, was different from the way she remembered him as a child. He wore a city suit and used a cane to favour his lame leg. His suit was of dark cloth and he no longer carried a Colt .45 holstered at his waist. Before, he had been a United States marshal; now he was one of the Commissioners.

She wasn't expecting much in the way of sympathy; he'd grown hard on the frontier, dealing out rough justice to gangs of desperadoes. He looked at her and took her into a saloon, sat her down and bought her a brandy.

'Get that down yuh, Jo. You look

frozen to hell and gone.'

She ignored the drinkers at the bar and the card players, and obeyed. The brandy burned her throat and warmed her body, but she was still ugly with hate and dead inside.

'Describe these men.'

She recited their names and descriptions as if she were ordering provisions at a store. 'All three had red hair.'

'Oh, yes, they're known — army deserters.' Uncle Lew used the term as a measure of contempt. 'I'll pass the word to my marshals to hunt them down.'

'They can pass the word to me,' said Jo McQueen. 'I'll do my own hunting. I'm going to kill them myself.' Her voice rose, attracting the attention of every man in the saloon. 'I'll trail them wherever they go no matter how long it takes, and I'll corner them like the rats they are and exterminate them. All three. One at a time, or all together.'

Lew watched her, then nodded, as if this were no more than he expected.

'I don't doubt yuh, Jo. It's an attitude bred into the bone right through our family. We pay our own debts, fight our own battles and take our own revenge.' He paused. 'Your parents were buried hastily, so I'll make myself responsible for a proper marker.'

He brought from his coat pocket a metal badge and a sheet of paper, which he filled in and signed.

'Raise your right hand and swear to uphold the United States law.' She obeyed mechanically, repeating the words after him. 'You are now a deputy US marshal, authorized to arrest these three men.'

'I don't need that stuff — I'm going to chase them down and kill them.'

'Of course you are, Jo. But the local law may not see it your way, and this covers you when they resist arrest. Put it in your pocket in case yuh need it.'

She obeyed, repeating in her head: Preacher, Solo, Fletch . . .

3

A Mexican Shave

Fletch rode a stolen army horse and that alone would be enough to get his neck stretched. It was a big black stallion, a fine animal with spirit.

He'd mostly got over his drink as he followed Solo and the Preacher across the prairie beneath a broiling sun. The homestead they'd stopped at was a vague memory.

Bleary-eyed, he took a swig from his water bottle, then poured a little liquid into his hand and rubbed it across the stubble on his jaw. The buttons of his army tunic had been ripped off and the length of his hair would have got him a reprimand on any parade ground. He smiled slyly; no one was ever going to get him on a parade ground again.

Joining the army as a youth — even to get away from home — had been a mistake. And so, now he thought of it, had been allowing himself to submit to the Preacher's power. True, the Preacher had the power to sway men's minds with his booming voice and carefully selected passages from the Bible. Fletch was ready to admit, finally, that he didn't like Preacher and wasn't that keen on Solo, whose interest in life was restricted to taking money off men at cards.

Preacher loved giving orders, so how was he any different from an officer in the army? To hell with him.

When you joined the army you had to put up with the men you served with; when you deserted, you didn't have to put up with anyone.

Fletch was getting around to thinking he might break loose from the other two. Somewhere nearby he had a cousin, according to a letter that had caught up with him in the last town they'd passed through; and the cousin was doing well running cattle. Other people's cattle. Reading between the lines, it appeared that Cousin Jack was working with a Mexican calling himself El Tigre. Waal, he didn't have anything against greasers if the money was there.

He realized that Preacher had turned his horse back to ride alongside.

'You're lagging, Fletch, and we need to distance ourselves from that homestead, just in case some busybody organizes a posse.'

'There ain't no one to tell on us.'

Preacher looked at him with a thoughtful expression. 'You should know — you were the last one out.'

'We agreed to make our break together, and stay together till we got clear of army units, that's all. Waal, we're clear.'

'That's so. Solo has mentioned he wants to stay on in the next town we hit, and try his skill at a card table.'

'And I've got a cousin in the cattle business, so maybe I'll join him.'

'Why not?'

'And you, Preacher? D'you have any plans?'

The Preacher raised his Bible, smiling. 'The Lord will provide,' he said, and rode forward to rejoin Solo.

Fletch lagged further behind, deliberately, until he lost sight of the pair. He didn't need either of them any longer. He was finished with the army, and one man could lose himself a lot easier than three.

Preacher had given him his last order. Fletch hated officers who gave him orders and backed them up with army punishment. He could still remember marching under a blazing sun with a sack of lead-shot on his shoulders. That bastard had paid; they might guess who shot him in the back but they couldn't prove it.

The hell with Preacher; he'd join Cousin Jack.

★ ★ ★

26

McQueen felt filthy when she rode in from drag position after helping to settle the cattle for the night, but there was no river to wash off the grime. She wiped her face with a damp rag, eased her parched throat with black coffee and forced herself to eat something. Washing would have to wait.

Wade glanced at her. 'You'll take your turn at night guard, McQueen. Two hours on.'

She nodded. If anyone thought she'd complain, they were disappointed and the men around the chuck wagon left her alone.

When she'd finished eating, Chester produced a bull whip only a little shorter than the one he used to control his mule team.

'Watch my wrist, missy. You need to understand the wrist action. Like this — ' he demonstrated, again and again. 'Try it.'

After a few attempts. she began to develop the knack of flicking her wrist.

Chester nodded approval. 'You're

almost there. Now it's a matter of getting your eye in.'

He pointed at a fly settling on the water barrel and showed how he controlled the whip to kill the fly without touching the barrel.

'If that barrel were a mule, missy, and you touched him, that animal would bolt. Start high and gradually, very gradually, get closer.'

She kept practising until her wrist ached and the light failed.

'Not bad,' Chester admitted. 'It needs a delicate touch, and you've got that. Remember, wrist and eye. Then it's practice, practice, practice.'

Jo McQueen kept at it.

* * *

Fletch didn't have a lot of patience, but he thought he'd better wait, despite the heat.

If Cousin Jack didn't show, he'd be on his own with no idea what he'd do in the future. He stood on top of what passed for a hill on the prairie, looking down at the trail. His stallion grazed nearby.

While he waited, he rolled a cigarette and lit up. Further down the hill was a clump of trees amid bare rocks. There would be shade there but his cousin had specified the top of the hill. Likely El Tigre wanted to make sure he was alone and that this meeting didn't turn out to be a trap.

That was fair enough, but he wished someone would make a move. He was getting hot and sweaty and losing patience fast.

A figure appeared, a man on foot coming up the hillside. Fletch studied him till he was sure it was Cousin Jack, then relaxed.

The moment he relaxed, the sharp point of a knife touched the back of his neck. He dropped his cigarette and froze.

His revolver was lifted from its holster and a smooth Mexican voice said. 'You are Fletch, sí? A cousin to one of my men, and you hope to join my band of brothers?'

'Yeah.'

Cousin Jack arrived, grinning broadly. 'You get the idea, Fletch? No one takes El Tigre by surprise — a real smart *hombre*.'

Fletch grunted, unhappy at having a Mexican behind him with a knife in his hand.

El Tigre prodded with the point of his blade. 'We shall see — walk down the hill, Fletch, to the shade. Jack, bring his horse.'

Fletch didn't like the way his options had just been wiped out, but it was only fair to warn his cousin. 'Watch the black — he can be a dangerous brute.' He moved down the grassy slope.

Among the trees was a smokeless fire, tethered horses, men drinking from bottles. He noticed one light a cheroot now he was in the bag; before there had been nothing to betray their presence.

Yes, he decided grudgingly, the Mexican was smarter than most. A couple of the gang now had guns in their hands.

'Sit, if you please, *señor*,' said El Tigre, indicating a flat rock beside the fire. Water bubbled in a tin can suspended over hot wood ash.

Fletch seated himself and got his first full view of the bandit chief. Anyone less like a tiger would be hard to imagine; he was fat; he waddled; his face was creased in a jolly smile. He wore flamboyant clothes trimmed with silver and a high sombrero.

But the knife still in his hand reminded Fletch that, indeed, El Tigre had teeth.

A man came up each side of Fletch and took an arm and held him firmly.

'Hi, Jack, what is this?'

Cousin Jack winked. 'Relax. It's a sort of initiation, is all.' But Fletch didn't like being handled.

El Tigre, still smiling, urged, 'Yes, relax, Fletch. That is good advice. Do not move your head by the smallest amount. Keep very still, *sí*?'

31

The Mexican dipped a bar of soap in hot water and rubbed it over the bristles on Fletch's face, working up a lather.

'I do not want any of my men to appear like a desert rat, señor, so I take upon myself the duty of barbering, sí?'

He snatched a hair from Fletch's head to test the edge of his knife and then began to shave the stubble from his face. Fletch went rigid.

'You see it now? A test of nerve, sí? Reflect how easy it would be for me to remove an ear ... take out an eye ... open your throat.'

Fletch remained still, his heart pounding. He'd never been so scared in his life — this fat Mexican could end it with a slip of his knife. And the bastard was obviously enjoying it. Despite the heat, he shivered as the blade pulled at his whiskers.

Sweat dripped into the lather while the men on each side of him gripped his arms and El Tigre wielded his homely razor. He was helpless, totally at the Mexican's mercy; but inside he raved and cursed.

His ordeal finally ended and El Tigre wiped his blade clean. The two men released him.

Fletch was trembling, half with fear, half with rage. He rubbed his face with his bandanna. His mouth was dry and Cousin Jack handed him a mug of coffee, and he swallowed.

The Mexican bandit smiled broadly.

'So now you are of my select band, señor. I trust you appreciate that while it was easy to desert from the United States' army, it is not so easy to leave El Tigre?'

The Mexican handed back his revolver and Fletch holstered it and nodded.

'Good. You are from the north, *si*?'

Fletch nodded again.

'That is well. It is history now, but the country known as Texas was stolen from my people by the Anglos even as they stole this land from the Indians. It was our *vaqueros* who taught Anglos how to rope cattle . . . so we take cattle from your trail drives and sell them to the Indian agents, *sí*?'

'Yeah.'

'This we do by stampeding the herds travelling north and helping ourselves.' El Tigre smiled pleasantly. 'It is easy enough when we have a man with the herd . . . '

* * *

Pike was taking it easy on his two-hour stint as a night guard, circling the herd already bedded down in the dark. He hummed quietly one of the popular songs of the day; most cowboys sang to their cattle — it seemed to relax them.

His opposite number, riding the reverse way around the resting animals approached. As they passed each other they signalled 'All's well'; nothing could be allowed to disturb the cows, who might spring to their feet and bolt. Sometimes the least thing would set them off.

The air was warm, stars winked between slowly drifting cloud. Alone, Pike brooded. He must have been loco even thinking of taking this kind of job for thirty a month; a job with little rest, poor food and no time off. That was why he'd pushed his luck with McQueen.

And the damned bitch had played hard to get. Christ, she'd really scared him for a minute; and that didn't look good in front of the crew. Crazy woman!

But at least he'd got away from drag position — she was eating dust now.

He reckoned she'd act differently if he had a roll of bills to flash in her face; he'd bet she'd change her tune then.

He cursed McQueen under his breath. Pike was still young enough to believe he was entitled to the good life, that he was destined for better things than trail driving. All he needed was the money to set himself up and . . . wa'al, he'd soon have that.

He smiled at the thought of what was

to come. It was only this thought that kept him going. Not much longer, he figured, to the rendezvous point; then Wade could chase his own cows.

Pike would be taking his ease in the best hotel a trail town could offer; after a hot bath and clean duds, good food and fine wine, he didn't doubt he'd find a willing woman.

Maybe he'd set up in business. Maybe take a partner. Yep, any time now.

4

Hoofs and Horns

The man she was due to relieve was wary about getting too close; he lightly tapped McQueen's shoulder with a long twig. Her eyes snapped open, staring at him.

'Night guard,' he called softly.

'Right.'

She came to her feet and dragged her saddle towards a cowpony. 'How are they?'

'Restless. If they run, keep clear.'

She nodded, and he vanished towards his bedroll. The sky was dark with cloud, the air humid as she saddled up and rode slowly out towards the herd.

She didn't mind night duty. It broke up her nightmare and helped reduce it to something she could control; fear left her and anger fanned the flame of vengeance. The trail drive was slow but, all the while, she was moving steadily north, the way the deserters had taken. And she was slowly learning that not all men were her natural enemy.

Chester was almost a friend, almost trusted. When she'd completed her after-supper practice with the bull whip he'd been complimentary. Then he'd looked at the gathering clouds and sniffed the air and warned her.

'Take care, missy. Could be a storm tonight.'

Not far off, her opposite number crooned an old favourite; 'Dinah had a wooden leg'. She'd heard that cows liked it, but she didn't feel like crooning to anyone or anything at the moment.

She rode silently around the herd. Big eyes followed her, making her uneasy. Occasionally a steer would rise, turn around and stand staring into the night before settling down again. The air held a tension she couldn't understand, but which she sensed in her blood.

An hour passed by the movement of the stars, and she began to look forward to her relief. Maybe tonight she would be able to rest without the nightmare returning.

Stars shone through breaks in the cloud and she glimpsed a rider going away from her, hoofbeats muffled. It was young Pike; she couldn't mistake that one, but he wasn't on night guard at the same time as her; Wade had insisted on that. So what was he doing riding the range at night?

McQueen didn't understand it, but suspicions grew in her head. He was not a man she was ever going to trust. She stared after him in the darkness until she lost sight of him, and looked around for the other night guard.

She heard gunshots, three, close together. Cattle came to their knees, then sprang upright. She cursed, and urged her pony to move further out from the herd. Shouts echoed, hoofs thundered.

She saw riders beating their hats on

their thighs and flicking the ends of lariats, shooting into the earth near to cows' feet. Steers milled about, uncertain, then the leaders ran and the rest followed.

She guessed now that Pike was working with some rustlers, splitting the herd to make it easy to run off a bunch. She rode on the outside, trying to reach the leaders to head them off; to be caught inside a running herd could be dangerous, even lethal.

She knew the theory; she leaned against the leading steers to turn them in a circle until they milled and finally came to a halt.

She glimpsed another rider ahead and swung towards him; he had a revolver in his hand and shot at her.

McQueen was taken by surprise and swung away again; obviously she'd caught up with one of the cattle thieves.

At a safer distance, she drew her rifle from its scabbard and returned fire. The rustler took off in a hurry, driving a bunch of cows before him.

Another horseman passed by at a gallop; this time she recognized one of Wade's cowhands. He bawled at her, 'Turn 'em *right*, and stay *left*.'

But steers were scattering at a dead run, hoofs rumbling, horns flashing like bayonets and just as deadly. It began to seem an impossible task.

Suddenly there were more men around her; all hands, including Wade and Chester, were in the saddle and trying to regain control.

Together they got most of the herd bunched and turning. She rode alongside the trail boss, shouting, 'Rustlers! One shot at me.'

'Forget 'em! We've got the largest part of the herd — let the others go.'

McQueen was beginning to think she might be able to relax when the storm broke. The wind came suddenly, lashing rain into her face. Thunder boomed like a barrage from heavy artillery, and the cattle spooked and bolted again.

It was all to do over, she thought with a sinking heart; it was going to be a long night. She put her pony to the gallop to catch up with the leaders.

Lightning zigzagged, turning the land a bilious green. The wind lifted her hat and only the chinstrap saved it. Slanting rain almost blinded her. Every time a lightning flash stabbed the ground, the cows panicked once more in a mad rush.

They ran silently, the ground trembling beneath their massed hoofs. She saw a vast sea of ridged backs, horns and tails that filled the night, and heard horns clash as they dashed headlong in blind panic, stumbling and swaying and crashing in the dark.

'Damn, damn, and damn,' McQueen muttered. 'Just when we had things back under control.'

Her cowpony moved like clockwork and she held the reins lightly. The cattle ran with a speed that surprised her, nose to tail.

The temperature dropped sharply. The air stank of ozone and lightning seemed to spark eerily from horn to horn. She no longer needed a bath; her clothes were soaked, water running over and down her body as if she were riding through a waterfall.

The humidity made her sweat. Thunder rolled incessantly. The sky was abnormally black, flickering as though a dark curtain was being blown backwards and forwards. Big drops of rain stung as they hit. She heard a horse scream in terror.

It was a frightful ride, the cattle at full run. A few steers went down, trapped in the crush, their footing lost. Their plaintive bellowing was cut off as they were trampled into the earth. Still the headlong rush continued and she kept to the outside, relying on her pony's sure-footing for her life.

The lightning was almost continuous, giving an eerie half-light like some supernatural glow, flaring up to an intense blue-white brilliance and fading again. She saw she had almost caught up with the rustlers.

The main herd was again treading on

the heels of those cattle Pike had separated off for the thieves. Still the stampede ran its course, and McQueen remembered she hadn't warned the trail boss about Pike.

She tried to turn her mount to get alongside Wade, but the pony wasn't interested; it was up with the leaders and leaning in to start another mill.

She shouted, but thunder drowned out her voice; rain came down like a sheet of water, hampering vision. Only when lightning flashed could she pick out any individual — this time a rustler ahead — and recognize him. The shock of surprise nearly unseated her. He'd lost his hat to the wind and his red hair glowed; she stared at the face of the man called Fletch.

He looked different from the memory seared into her mind, but she had no doubt. He still wore the army tunic without buttons, and the face was the one she saw in her nightmare, a face she would never forget.

Hatred surged through her like a

huge shot of pure energy. She came alert with the need for revenge burning like a flame inside her. It was a furious anger threatening to consume her.

She forgot the herd, Wade, Chester, Pike, the rustlers. Only Fletch existed in her world, here and now, he existed as a target to be destroyed.

She forced her pony away from the running cattle; it faltered, trying to get back to a job it knew, then it grasped her intention and McQueen settled down to hunt Fletch.

He, too, appeared to be on his own for the moment and she knew she had to reach him before he rejoined the gang. He seemed to be concentrating on keeping a bunch of steers going the way he wanted them to go.

She laid her rifle across her pony's neck and loosed off a shot. She missed, but the bullet was close enough to make him look round. He drew his revolver and fired, but the lead was lost in the wind and rain.

Obviously he didn't recognize her,

just assumed she was one of the cowhands driving the herd to Kansas. He wasn't bothered. Why should he be? Wade's men were only interested in getting their runaway herd together; he never dreamt she was his personal nemesis.

She saw the gunflash as he fired again; a warning shot. But her pony was tiring and the big black stallion Fletch rode was moving steadily away. Lightning forked, and she threw one last slug after him.

Another miss, but close enough to make the big horse swerve, and a long curved horn gored Fletch's leg. The cow tossed its head, lifting him out of the saddle. He would have fallen, but one foot caught in a stirrup.

As the black horse raced to get clear of storm-crazed animals, Fletch was dragged, helpless, along the ground.

He struggled to get a grip on the stirrup leather to haul himself up, but couldn't find the strength as cows continually jostled him. He tried to keep himself above the ground, beyond the reach of pounding hoofs, but blood still ran from his leg, weakening him.

Then he seemed to slump, perhaps giving up in despair, perhaps losing consciousness, then relaxed his hand-hold and was dragged along, face down in the mud.

The cattle ran, and the black horse ran with them for endless miles and Jo McQueen, grim-faced, followed. Rain hammered down and the wind howled. Thunder drummed and lightning was like green-tinged fire. Time lost all meaning in the roar of hoofs, driving rain and gusting wind.

When the storm finally died, just before dawn, the cattle slowed and Fletch's horse broke clear and came to a standstill, quivering, breathing hard. Its rider lay motionless, a lump of raw meat.

McQueen reined in her pony and almost fell from the saddle, holding to the horn to stay upright. The sun's first rays peeped through the cloud, tinting the land red. It was strangely quiet, with a few cows lying down and no sign of rustlers or cattlemen.

She walked on wobbly legs towards the body, water draining from her clothes. Her boots squelched as she covered the flooded ground, breaking the silence.

What was left of Fletch could be left for the vultures. One of the faces she had thought she would never forget had been obliterated. There were a few shreds of reddish hair, half buried in mud, to indicate who it had been.

McQueen turned away with no feeling of satisfaction. She felt she had been cheated of her revenge.

5

A Town Called Hope

Solo liked to dress the way a cowboy dressed because it disarmed his victims. They thought he was one of them and weren't so likely to treat him as a cardsharp when he took their wages off them.

He rode with Preacher towards the town showing on the horizon under a scorching sun. Even though they'd sought what shade and water there was, they were both dried out like prunes. Both horses were close to collapsing.

A meal, he thought, with a gallon of water; a bath and a change of clothes to shake out the dust — then he'd find a saloon and a poker game. He was beginning to think Fletch had the right idea; split from the Preacher and go it alone.

The trouble with Preacher, he decided, was that he considered himself ordained to give orders. Solo hated taking orders and discipline; that was why he'd quit the army without waiting for an official discharge. He, too, had experienced army punishment, designed to humiliate and intimidate.

Preacher talked big and had big ideas, while all Solo wanted was a game of cards where he came out ahead, making enough money so he never had to do hard work. Since Fletch had broken free, he bore the brunt of the Preacher's authoritarian pronouncements.

As they approached the town, he was reaching the point the army would have called mutiny. Someone had put up a wooden post and painted a name he found encouraging: HOPE, it read.

Solo rode along the main street, Broadway, with a lighter heart. There didn't seem to be many people about but, further on, he saw a wagon hitched outside a store, a couple of horses at a water trough, a saloon and false-fronted dining-room. And a body lying in the road.

Apparently no one was bothered enough to remove it. He brightened: 'Looks like my kind of town.'

Preacher didn't seem impressed. 'There are doubtless many sinners, but where are the men of property? One bank, and I see that is closed. Other shops appear to have shut down. I think this can be no more than a stopover for rest and food.'

'Figure I'll find myself a saloon with a game going and stay a while.'

'As you choose. I shall ride on in the morning. I have a craving for a larger amount of money than is likely to be available here. For the Lord's work, of course.'

'Of course.'

'Take note, Solo, of the building opposite.'

He glanced across the street to a door labelled *Sheriff's Office*.

As he looked, a man stepped out; a very large man, giving the impression he was almost as wide as he was tall; a giant, moving with slow deliberation. He collected a handcart from a shed which he pushed along the dusty street to the body. Then he picked up the corpse without apparent effort, placed it in the cart and wheeled it towards the end of the town.

The Preacher made a rare smile. 'It would seem the office of lawman and undertaker are combined.'

He pulled over and hitched his horse outside a two-storey building advertised as a 'Boarding and Lodging House', and went inside.

Solo hesitated before continuing along Broadway. He'd changed his mind, he had to get away from the Preacher; a bath and change of clothes would have to wait. He felt the need for a drink and stopped at the first open saloon. *Doc's Place* proclaimed faded paint above the bat wings.

He bought a beer for twenty-five cents, gulped it down and bought another. He leaned against the counter, surveying the tables. There was not much action so far; low stakes, but it was early yet.

He didn't see any problems until two men walked in. They stood just inside the doorway, studying the room and and its occupants; then they crossed the sawdust floor and approached the bar.

The one in the lead was thickset with bulging muscles and a beard like a dark bush; he had a big hooked nose and looked as if he could be very unpleasant if he chose to be.

'I'm Kummer,' he said, 'and I run this town. I haven't seen you before, Red. Just passing through or thinking of staying?'

'Looking for a job,' Solo lied. 'D'yuh reckon there's a ranch around here looking for a hand, Mr Kummer?'

'I know nothing about ranching.'

Solo was keenly aware of the second man; slim and lightweight, he stood poised with one gun at his hip and his hand resting on the butt. Kummer might fancy himself as the town boss, but this was the dangerous one; probably fast and accurate.

'Maybe I'll sit in on a poker game,' he said smoothly, and Kummer held out his hand and demanded five bucks.

'For what?'

'Taxes. You stay in town, you pay tax. I'll collect now or Henry here'll run you outa town his way.'

'The sheriff know about this?'

Kummer laughed, a sneering sound. 'Baldwin's too old for anything. He keeps out of my way.'

'Looked big to me,' Solo said. 'You sure you ain't joshing me?'

'Sounds like you saw his deputy. Real slow up top — by the time he's caught on what's happening, it's all over.'

'Guess I'll pay your tax,' Solo said grudgingly, and counted out the money.

'Welcome to Hope, Red. Enjoy your stay.'

Kummer moved along to the bartender. Henry stared at Solo for several seconds, as if his eyes were photographing his face for reference.

After Henry moved on, Solo watched a poker school until one of the players dropped out and he was invited into the game.

★ ★ ★

Sheriff Baldwin stood by the window of his house, looking out at the town he had been appointed to police. He watched Robbie, his deputy, wheel a corpse away to plant on Boot Hill. He was feeling depressed; his deputy shouldn't have to do that, but since Kummer and his gang had moved in and taken over, everything had gone downhill.

Playing second fiddle to a bunch of crooks was not what he'd signed up for, but he was getting old and knew he was too slow to take out Kummer's man-killer.

But it wasn't only age. He got no support because many of the townsfolk had given up and moved away. He felt like changing the town's name to Hopeless.

Those left seemed content to make money from the outlaws; saloonkeepers, gamblers and whores. Or, like himself, were too old to make an objection stick. Shops continued to shut, giving that part of the town a dead look. The only big store left, the Three Star Emporium, was the one Kummer patronized. Each day, a few more citizens quit; soon the place would be only another roost for robbers. It was humiliating to be a lawman in Hope.

His wife, Amy, joined him at the window. 'It's not right Robbie should have to clean up after those scum.'

It was a pity they'd never managed to start a family; childless, she thought of his deputy as the son they'd both wanted.

Baldwin sighed. 'I agree, dear, but show me an alternative. If dead bodies were simply left around, we'd all go down with some sickness. And 'cause he's a bit weak in the head, Kummer leaves him alone.' He added, with some bitterness, 'Because I'm old and past it, he doesn't bother with me either.'

'In the old days —— '

'The old days!' Baldwin turned from the window. Amy's face was lined with worry, her hair tied back in a bun, partly grey. 'Back then I'd have showed Henry the inside of a jail. I'd have had the backing of solid citizens. Where are they now?'

'You can't blame them for getting out when a gang of ruffians takes over and demands money for not wrecking their shops and business.'

'Maybe not . . . and maybe I can. I reckon those who appoint a lawman should stand behind him when necessary. It's too late now.' He sighed. 'I'm just a joke.'

'Not to me, Bert, so stay out of trouble. I'm not yet ready to be made a widow.'

★　★　★

Preacher stepped out of the boarding-house after a refreshing bath and a change of clothing. He stood a moment, Bible under his arm, looking both ways. He'd enquired of the landlady where he might procure a meal, and she'd recommended the dining-room across the street.

But first he walked his horse to the livery stable and ordered the animal to be rubbed down, fed and housed until morning.

The town appeared dead and confirmed his decision to move on. One store remained open, a few saloons, and they seemed unusually quiet. Preacher frowned, wondering if the sheriff had a tighter grip on the town than he'd assumed. It crossed his mind that Solo might regret his choice.

He entered the dining room, chose an empty table near the window and ordered from the menu. He sat watching and listening.

He could have eaten at the lodging house but preferred to take the temperature of the town. When his food arrived — a slab of pork, potatoes and canned tomatoes — he ate slowly, the Bible on the table beside his plate.

Two cowpunchers ate at one table, apparently subdued. A man and wife, middle-aged, at another, both looking down. Conversation was limited.

Two men entered and walked up to the counter, and the woman gave them money; she didn't appear happy about it, just resigned. They stopped beside his table.

'New in town, Reverend?' asked the one with a big hooked nose. 'Thinking of staying?'

'Overnight. I shall be moving on in the morning.'

The man nodded. 'In that case, I'll excuse yuh. We find most folk like to pay their taxes as soon as they hit town. Taxes to help maintain the town's amenities, Reverend.'

Preacher looked blandly at him, then studied the second man. 'I shall,' he said, 'intercede with the Lord on your behalf. That is worth more than any mite I could contribute to your worthy fund.'

The two men exchanged a glance, and left. The husband and wife sighed quietly.

Outside, Henry frowned. 'Not a good idea, boss. Let one off and they'll all be demanding you excuse them.'

Kummer smiled thinly. 'Then I'll expect you to disabuse them of that notion. Coming down heavy on a man of the cloth is not a good idea. It could stir people up, Henry, when what we want is a mood of quiet resignation.'

★ ★ ★

El Tigre surveyed the small bunch of cattle his men had managed to collect, and sadly shook his head. The night raid had not been a success. He looked at a couple of bedraggled men trying to get a fire going.

'I blame no one,' he said generously. 'Not even I could foretell a storm of such intensity. I doubt if those trail drivers have had any more luck in gathering cattle — the beasts must be scattered over many, many miles by now.

'This bunch,' he indicated the few steers lying down in attitudes that suggested they might be reluctant ever to get up again, 'will pay for a trip to town, a few drinks, perhaps an hour with a woman. No more. Next time . . . perhaps we need a change of tactics.'

Cousin Jack looked sourly at him. 'Tactics?'

'I am sorry about your relation, Jack — and on his first outing with us too — but in a stampede it is each man for himself, as you know.'

Jack merely nodded. It was Fletch's black horse he'd coveted, and that had simply gone missing.

El Tigre looked at his youngest recruit and laid a fatherly hand on his shoulder.

'In this life, *amigo*, there are many disappointments, but we shall together overcome them. There is little money to share this time, but the next

61

. . . who knows?'

Pike scowled. His chance at big money to spend on every luxury he could imagine had vanished, to be replaced by an uncertain life outside the law. And he wasn't even sure he liked this fat Mexican.

El Tigre brooded as he waited hopefully for a mug of coffee.

'It seems that rustling is no longer a worthwhile operation. Kummer, a cheap no-good, has done better simply by taking over a small town and running it to suit himself. Of course, he depends on a gunman — the one who calls himself Henry — and is nothing without him.'

El Tigre surveyed his defeated men and smiled encouragingly.

'It occurs to me we might remove Henry first, and then Kummer, and make Hope our town. Does that appeal to anyone?'

Several faces brightened. It seemed the idea had more appeal than trying to light a fire to boil coffee.

6

Death of a Man-Killer

US deputy marshal Yale awoke refreshed after six hours sleep under the sky. His horse grazed peacefully beside the trail. He splashed water from a creek over his face and made a fire to cook breakfast; he was headed into unknown country and a full stomach seemed a good idea.

He put water in a can to boil and squatted, slicing bacon into a pan and adding yesterday's leftover beans. Rolling his first cigarette of the day, he watched the sun rise over a small town in the valley below. An early rider was coming up the trail at a leisurely pace, and Yale eased the Colt revolver in his holster.

The town was no concern of his, but he'd heard rumours, and he was a small man of mild appearance. The rider approached and he saw a cowboy with a glum expression on a pony. The rider paused, looking hungrily at his breakfast and sniffing appreciation.

''Light and eat, fellar,' Yale called, pouring coffee and slicing more bacon.

The cowboy's face brightened. 'Sure will,' he drawled, 'and thanks. Sat in a poker game last night and got cleaned out. Not even enough for breakfast before riding back to the bunkhouse. You're a lifesaver.'

Yale offered him the makings. 'Guess you met one of them cardsharps.'

'Sure didn't look it.' The cowboy smoked his cigarette. 'Dressed just like one of us.'

Yale came alert, remembering a message from Commissioner Lewis. 'Heard tell there was one like that around, fellar with red hair.'

'Sounds like the same gent — calls himself Solo. Haven't seen him here before.' The cowboy paused to demolish the food Yale handed him, wiping the pan with a chunk of bread. 'Going into town?'

'Heading west.'

'Wa'al, I advise bypassing Hope. Place is run by a bunch of crooks.'

Yale shrugged. 'I've no reason to bother them. Expecting to cross a cattle trail someplace.'

The cowboy drained the mug and prepared to swing into his saddle. 'Keep riding west and you'll hit it — and thanks again.' He mounted and rode on.

Yale brought a stub of pencil from his shirt pocket and sucked the end while he composed a message in his head. Writing was not something he did every day and it took thought. Finally, with some care, he wrote his message on the back of an old envelope.

When he'd washed his pan and mug in the creek, he continued his journey. The message in his pocket had nothing to do with his current assignment; it was addressed to McQueen.

★ ★ ★

When McQueen arrived back at the chuck wagon after the storm; she was riding a big black stallion and leading a cowpony. She felt wet, tired and depressed.

Chester beamed a big smile as he handed her a tin mug filled to the brim with sweet black coffee. 'Glad to see you made it back, missy. Food coming up right away.'

She saw cowhands sprawled on the ground, looking beat from an all-night chase. No one had a lot to say; there were still missing cows to locate and drive into the herd.

Wade glanced at the stallion with interest. 'Got yourself a real horse there, McQueen.'

She nodded. 'Belonged to a rustler, but he's no further use for it.'

'Makes up for young Pike, I suppose. He didn't make it back.'

A memory stirred. 'Pike sold you out, Mr Wade. He was running off cattle for the rustlers. He may still be with them.'

Wade's expression changed. 'The hell

you say! If I meet him again I'll stretch his neck.'

Chester handed her a tin plate filled with stew and newly baked biscuits. 'Get this down yuh, missy.' She wasn't hungry but knew he was right; she needed to get something hot inside her.

When she'd finished eating, he offered her an old envelope, folded over. 'Fellar came by earlier and left this for yuh.'

She opened it out and read: *A man with red hair calling himself Solo was in a poker game in Hope.*

She didn't know the handwriting but it was initialled, *W.Y. (deputy marshal)*

Chester watched her face change. The tiredness disappeared. She quivered like a hunting dog that had scented its quarry, and he felt glad he was not the person she was so obviously thinking about.

Solo, number two on her list, in Hope. And the question nagging at the back of her mind was answered; yes, Uncle Lew was going to help.

She pushed the empty plate back at the negro cook. 'Thanks for everything, Chester.'

She grabbed her bedroll from the chuck wagon and tied it behind her saddle. 'Leaving you now, Mr Wade.'

He nodded, perhaps not as glad to see her go as he would have been before.

The big black stallion she had named Nemesis took the trail to Hope.

* * *

It was close to midday when Solo aired himself on a bench outside Doc's Place.

A couple of dogs drowzed on the boardwalk; a few older citizens scurried home after shopping and before Kummer's men started patrolling. He wondered if his stomach would accept food yet when a horseman passed by — Preacher, wearing black and carrying his Bible.

Solo lifted a hand in greeting and farewell, but Preacher ignored him. We might never have ridden the same trail, he thought; so good riddance! The horseman continued along Broadway, heading out of town.

'It's not often,' a voice boomed in his ear, 'that you see a red-haired preacher.'

Solo jumped. He hadn't seen the small man approach. Neatly dressed, his head was hairless and his voice the biggest thing about him.

'Sorry if I startled you. I forget I don't have to make my voice carry these days. No sir, not any more. Just plain forgot that.'

Solo gave him a quick look-over. Clean-shaven, the newcomer appeared prosperous from his dress; but Solo remained wary. Word had probably got around that he'd made a killing at poker last night.

'You're new in town,' the small man informed everybody within hearing, 'so I'll introduce myself.'

He jerked a manicured thumb in the direction of the saloon's name-sign.

'That's me, Doc Pomeroy. Kummer

will be around later to collect a tax on your winnings. If you're aiming to hang around town,' he looked questioningly at Solo, 'I can offer a piece of advice.'

'I'm listening.'

Doc's face shone. 'A pleasure to deal with a sensible man! Pay Kummer this time. One of my saloon gals has a shack outside the town limits and she's been known to rent it out. These days there's not a lot of action until the cowhands from the Double Cross show up on a Saturday night when, by coincidence, Kummer's gang keeps a low profile.

'So,' Pomeroy rubbed the side of his nose, 'if you were snugged in that gal's shack, you might ride in on a Saturday night and keep most of your winnings. Why hand more to that jackal than you need to?'

'Sounds good to me,' Solo said. 'Sure like to meet that gal and come to some arrangement.'

'Ask for Lizzie at the bar. She's usually around in the afternoon.'

'Guess you're no friend of Kummer.'

Pomeroy scowled. 'I was doing nicely until he arrived. I don't do badly now, but Kummer takes his cut and his gang expect free drinks. Hope ain't what it was.'

He looked Solo up and down.

'A bit more advice, seeing you're not above listening to someone old enough to be your father. It ain't just Kummer and his man-killer — he has a whole bunch of roughnecks who love beating up any opposition. So it pays to keep your nose clean.'

'You sure speak out loud and clear, Doc.'

'Yes, well, I used to be a patent medicine man. I've covered most of the West with a suitcase filled with pills and potions — I expect you've heard of Pomeroy's Balm and Regulator — something to cure any and everything. And you've got to put over the ballyhoo in that job.'

He smiled, reminiscing.

'My tonics worked — they always made you feel better, and so they should being fifty per cent alcohol. It came to me one day, like a revelation, how many more people I could help if I opened a saloon and dispensed the hundred per cent stuff. Works too. I was doing just fine until Kummer and his gang arrived.'

He nodded casually. 'Be seeing you, friend.'

'Thanks. Doc.'

As Pomeroy moved away, Solo stepped into the saloon in search of a health cure and Lizzie.

★ ★ ★

Henry sat watching Kummer feed his face in the hotel dining-room and was not impressed.

He ate too much and too fast, shovelling it in, reminding Henry of an animal at a trough. Henry felt contempt, but kept it from showing in his face. He sipped coffee from a cup and tried to change his boss's mind.

'You don't need Baldwin,' he argued,

'so let me take him out. Then you can appoint me sheriff and we're in the clear. I can declare anything legal. It'll be the perfect set-up.'

Kummer speared several pieces of bacon with his fork and shoved them in his mouth and chewed and talked around them.

'There's no need. Everything's running smooth as an oiled wheel, so why change a winning hand? Ignore Baldwin. He's old and past it, but he still makes a great figurehead. Any visitors come, it's obvious there's law in town and that covers us. No, Henry, leave him alone.'

Henry kept calm until he was outside the hotel. As he strode along the boardwalk, scowling, men got out of his path and women crossed the street to avoid him. His lip curled. He was used to this reaction even if he didn't understand it; he'd never backed away from anyone in his life.

His back trail, through town after town, was littered with bodies to prove it.

His earliest memories were of a hero who was fastest on the draw, and he'd practised for years until he became that man. He didn't need to back down because he could always draw first. It paid well too; a lot of so-called big men hired him. Like Kummer; he despised Kummer, but took his money and propped him up.

Still, being denied his chance to outdraw Baldwin festered like a concealed sore. He loathed lawmen; it seemed as if wherever he went, a lawman watched and waited for any chance to pick on him.

But if he were sheriff . . .

He saw Baldwin ahead, coming along the boardwalk towards him. The sheriff paused, as if considering ducking out of a confrontation. Henry smiled, and the sheriff came on. It seemed that Baldwin was giving him the excuse he needed.

'Get outa my way, you old has-been,' he said loudly.

Baldwin paused again. It was obvious he didn't want a fight, but there were people watching. If he turned away now, he'd lose his last vestige of authority.

'Get off the plankwalk, or draw!'

Henry's hand was poised over the butt of his Colt. The sheriff thought sadly of his wife, Amy, but couldn't find the courage to step aside while the town watched. He made up his mind and went into a gunfighter's crouch.

Henry sniggered. This was going to be the easiest kill he'd ever made . . .

* * *

Even though McQueen was in a hurry to reach Hope and find Solo before he moved on, she took time out to rest her horse. Nemesis was big and strong but, after running with stampeding cattle, he couldn't be considered fresh enough for an all-out effort.

She let him rest and graze on the way to town so that when they did arrive the stallion was livelier than when they'd set out. McQueen had a close-up image of Solo's face in her head and an urge to remake his acquaintance, this time over the sights of a rifle. She felt no need for a macho face-to-face duel; she just wanted to kill him to stop him murdering again.

Hope appeared quiet on the surface as she rode slowly along Broadway. Then she noticed the watchers in doorways and behind windows, and two men facing each other on the board-walk. Looked like there was to be a gunfight but, as neither man had red hair, she wasn't concerned. It meant nothing to her if men killed each other.

She rode casually towards them. One old, one young. The old one was a fool, she thought; naturally the young one had an edge. Then she saw that the old man wore a law badge.

Her memory stirred; Uncle Lew had made her swear to uphold the law. She urged her big horse closer to the boardwalk as she uncoiled the bull whip Chester had given her. She'd practised till her arm ached; now to see if she could use it for real.

'Get off the plankwalk, or draw!' the young one said.

The elderly sheriff went into a crouch, reaching for his revolver.

McQueen measured the distance with her eye, gripped the stock of the whip as she'd been taught, and sent the lash snaking out. The end curled around the young man's gun and snatched it from his hand as he squeezed the trigger. The shot went wild.

The sheriff fired and the man-killer went over backwards, blood staining his shirt.

In the silence, an admiring voice said, 'Smart, lady!'

She turned her head to face the biggest man she'd ever seen. He stood tall enough so their eyes were almost level as she sat her horse, and he was wide and thick to match. For a moment she knew panic, sensing that if he laid a hand on her, she'd be helpless. Then he gave a delighted smile and she noted the deputy sheriff's badge he wore.

He scooped up the gunman's revolver and stuck it in his belt. 'I'll happily bury this one, Bert.'

He caught hold of the dead man by a boot and dragged him off the board-walk to a handcart.

The sheriff reloaded his revolver and looked about before holstering it. He removed his Stetson to mop sweat from his face.

'Obliged to yuh, ma'am. Reckon yuh saved my life with that trick. Name's Baldwin.'

'McQueen.'

'My wife will want to thank yuh and, if you're looking for a place to stay in town, we'd be happy to let you have our spare room.'

'Thanks. I may have to stay a while.'

Baldwin resettled his hat. 'This way, ma'am.'

She rode alongside the sheriff to a neat frame building, slid from the saddle and hitched Nemesis. She carried her bedroll and rifle into the house.

There were wild flowers in a jar on a windowsill. A thin woman with grey hair in a bun hurried towards them. 'I heard shooting — '

'Amy,' the sheriff said, 'this young lady just saved my life. That gunman of Kummer's picked on me in public and I couldn't just run and — '

Amy's worried look vanished. The creases in her face smoothed out in a welcoming smile. She held out her hand.

'Please treat this house as your own, young lady.'

The sheriff sat down with a heavy sigh, lit a cheroot and inhaled deeply.

'Amy doesn't like me smoking indoors, but I feel funny, like a doctor suddenly gave me an extra lease on life . . . you saw my deputy arrive too late to help. He was all right when Hope was a quiet town, before Kummer's gang moved in. He's still all right if it's a matter of escorting a drunk to the jail. For anything else . . . ' Baldwin shook his head sadly.

Amy protested, 'You're not being fair, Bert. Robbie's just a bit slow, is all.'

McQueen saw her look at the hunting knife at her belt, but all she said was, 'Drop your gear in the back room while I heat water for a bath. Then you'll eat with us. I'm Amy — what name do I call you?'

'McQueen's fine.'

The sheriff got to his feet. 'I'll leave you two to get acquainted while I walk the black to the livery stable.'

'Watch the stallion, Sheriff. He can be ugly with strangers.'

Outside, Baldwin muttered, 'He's not the only one. I wonder how Kummer's going to take this?'

7

Take-over

Frank Kummer was enjoying a free glass of the best brandy in Doc's Place when one of his men hurried in. A glance at Ike's face told him that something was seriously wrong.

'What is it?'

'Henry wasn't fast enough. The sheriff beat him to the draw and he's dead.'

'Henry?' Kummer couldn't quite take it in. 'The sheriff? I find that hard to believe.'

'There's no doubt about it. That big deputy's digging Henry's grave right this minute.'

Kummer swore. 'Damn it, I told him to leave Baldwin alone. The law wasn't bothering us.'

Ike signalled the bartender for a

whiskey. When it was poured he tossed it back in a single gulp. 'What happens now, boss? Henry had this town running scared.'

Kummer saw the customers looking his way, ears strained. Doc Pomeroy smiled blandly.

'Nothing changes,' he said quickly. 'I own this town . . . but how the hell did it happen?'

'Didn't see it myself, boss. The talk is a woman rode into town and helped the sheriff.'

'A woman?'

Kummer thought this even more unlikely than Baldwin beating Henry to the draw. Perhaps it was the heat? Or the brandy? Nothing seemed to make sense any more.

'Goddamn it, I'd better look into this myself.'

He finished his brandy in one swallow and pushed through the bat wings. There were more townsfolk on the street than he'd seen lately, and they were all staring at him, waiting to see what he'd do. He was the focus of attention in Hope.

He stood on the boardwalk, stroking his beard. Well, what was he going to do? He had other gunslingers, but no one the calibre of Henry. That was when doubt set in . . .

★ ★ ★

McQueen was beginning to feel halfway human again; a bath in hot clean water, she found, made that much difference. And the smell and taste of home-cooking . . . then suddenly she remembered how her mother had died and tightened up inside.

Solo was somewhere here and he was next on her list; she could not relax until she'd got him in her sights.

The sheriff's wife sighed. 'Whatever it is bothering you, I wish you'd take Robbie with you while you're here. He's — '

'No. I don't rely on any man.' What

she meant was 'I can't trust any man.'

They were washing dishes in the kitchen after the meal, and Amy tried again.

'You're hard for one so young. Robbie would never hurt a woman, or allow one to be hurt. He's one of nature's gentlemen, and big and strong. Even the scum ruining this town walk carefully around him.'

So would I, McQueen thought, remembering his size.

'Bert's a bit prejudiced because, well, I've got to admit, Robbie's a bit slow on the uptake. But he's willing to do anything to please — you just tell him what you want and he'll do it. Make no mistake about this: he could be a big help to you.'

McQueen was beginning to realize Hope was no ordinary town. Reluctantly, she agreed she might allow the big deputy to escort her around.

'I'm hunting for a man with red hair,' she told him when he returned from Boot Hill.

Robbie smiled happily; the young lady who'd saved the sheriff wanted him to help her. If he'd been a dog, he'd have wagged his tail.

As they walked down Broadway together, he looked carefully at each man's head. There was a noticeable lack of men with red hair, until they came to the Three Star Emporium; then a man wearing a Derby stepped out on to the boardwalk.

Long hair strayed from under the hat and Robbie covered the distance in easy strides, flipped off the hat to reveal a head of fiery red hair.

'Got him!' he shouted.

'Hey, what d'yuh think you're doing?' protested the man as Robbie half-carried, half-dragged him across the street to her.

'Your man with red hair,' he said proudly. 'I got him real quick!'

'Is this guy crazy?' the redhead protested. 'Sure I've got red hair — so have lots of other men. Is that a crime now?'

McQueen frowned. This man was obviously older than Solo as she remembered him. Robbie had made a mistake — or she had in not being clear enough.

'You can let him go, Robbie. He's not the one I'm looking for.'

Robbie was upset. 'But he's got red hair!'

'Yes, he has,' she sighed. 'I can see that, but he's still not the one I'm looking for.'

Dejected, Robbie released his grip.

Reluctantly, she said, 'Sorry, mister.' She hated having to apologize to a man. 'Robbie was trying to help me. It's my fault. Sorry.'

The redhead snorted and stalked away to reclaim his hat.

'My fault, Robbie, not yours. The one I'm after . . .

She described Solo, remembering all the while that Preacher was putting distance between them.

★ ★ ★

Preacher was not hurrying his horse; he didn't think the army would be pursuing him this far. But he avoided big towns where there might be a telegraph office; news circulated faster in such places.

The army had been useful for a time; easy enough for a wanted man to hide under a number and false name, but enough was enough. Preacher approved of discipline when he applied it to others; it lost its savour when the army applied it to him.

He had almost forgotten Fletch and Solo. Neither were his choice of company; useful allies, perhaps, when deserting, but no more than that. Preacher considered himself superior; he should have been an officer but the army didn't see him that way. Their loss, of course.

For the present he was content to visit lonely homesteads, where his garb as a man of religion ensured him a meal, and sometimes more. Women appeared to enjoy tempting him into sin. A collection from a small congregation was always useful.

He kept to high ground, watchful. Sometimes he confused himself, almost believed his own words. As a leader of an army of the Lord he would be wealthy, powerful.

Once he saw a New Pacific express winding its way between wooded hills and thought about robbing it. He'd heard that trains sometimes carried bullion; a big haul meant he could relax in comfort for a while, perhaps months.

He'd need information, and helpers. He never doubted his ability to plan a successful hold-up.

He crossed a shallow river and, in late evening, was considering where to lay his head for the night when the fiery glow of sunset silhouetted a building high on a hilltop. Could be anything, he thought, and watched till the light faded. No lamps showed. The air remained silent. Intriguing.

He urged his horse on, following a circuitous path upwards. It took longer to reach than he'd anticipated, and he approached cautiously.

When finally he arrived he saw only ruins of what was left; the building was unoccupied, but it had been an army fort before being abandoned. He explored it by moonlight and the more he studied its situation, the more he liked it.

This was a stronghold in an out-of-the-way place, perhaps forgotten. As a hideout, it promised well. Preacher smiled and murmured, 'Thank you, Lord. I have a vision . . .'

★ ★ ★

Solo was seated at a table shuffling and cutting cards, dealing them smoothly and fast when Lizzie came into the shack.

It was a one-room affair, half of it curtained off with a blanket for a sleeping place; it had a crudely fashioned table and wooden boxes for chairs, a fireplace for cooking and a creek nearby to provide water.

What set it apart from others of its kind was a screen of trees discreetly hiding it from the trail going into and out of Hope. This made it useful for men who didn't want to advertise their presence.

She said sharply, 'How come some young woman's looking for you, Solo?'

He looked up and grinned. 'Guess I'm just naturally popular with the ladies.'

'I doubt that. This one looks more like she'll stick a knife in yuh. Or a slug. She's carrying a rifle, and that big deputy's along with her.'

Solo began to take her a bit more seriously. There had been so many women, in none of whom he had any further interest. He shrugged and began to lay out the cards again.

'I've no idea, Liz. Guess I'll just have to keep out of her way.'

'You'd better. Since he planted Henry, Robbie's been like her shadow.'

Lizzie put a small bottle on the table.

'Don't drink this . . . apparently she's after a redhead.'

'What is it?'

'It's what we women use when our hair begins to look — you know — not quite so young.'

Solo looked at her with interest. A big blonde, a bit worn but still serviceable. 'So?'

'A dye. This one will turn your hair a sort of browny colour.'

He frowned. 'You think that's necessary?'

'I'm a business woman and I aim to save enough to start my own house one day. This will save trouble when you come into town to play cards. You win, you pay me. A dead man is a poor investment, and I don't want any young woman interfering with our arrangement.'

Solo shrugged. 'Guess I'll use your dye.'

★ ★ ★

McQueen patrolled Broadway, looking into each diner, saloon and hotel. She felt she was wasting time and energy, and was feeling frustrated. There was no sign of her quarry anywhere.

After a while she realized that if Solo was a cardsharp she might have to wait till evening to see if he turned up. Or the weekend.

Robbie trailed along behind her, quiet after his mistake. Now he said, 'Mr Kummer is here.'

McQueen turned. She'd learned he was boss of the gang who employed Henry, but wasn't bothered one way or the other. If he left her alone, she'd ignore him. It was Solo she wanted.

Kummer took up most of the boardwalk with armed men flanking him, one on each side. He wore an expensive suit and had a hooked nose above a bush of a beard. He halted, facing her in front of the Three Star Emporium.

'Is that right what I hear? That you helped the sheriff kill Henry?'

McQueen countered. 'Is that right what I hear? That you ordered Henry to gun down the sheriff?'

'No, it isn't. I told the fool to leave Baldwin alone.'

'Then we've no quarrel. I'm not interested in you unless you get in my way.' Casually, she swung the muzzle of her rifle up till it pointed at Kummer's stomach.

His men inched forward, watching her, hands dropping to the butts of their revolvers. Robbie growled warningly and clenched his hands. A bead of sweat gathered on Kummer's forehead then trickled down his face. He looked sick.

'I admire your courage, young lady, but — '

A figure waddled from the store doorway immediately behind Kummer. A fat figure wearing a tall sombrero; it moved silently.

Sunlight glinted briefly on the blade of a knife, and Kummer shuddered. He stopped speaking and stumbled forward, twisting around in an attempt to look behind him. He collapsed on the plankwalk, and his men stared down, not quite believing their eyes.

A Mexican waved a bloody knife and laughed.

'*Amigos*,' he said cheerfully. 'Look around before you make a fatal mistake. Do you not see many guns pointed your way? Know that I am El Tigre, and I am now the boss man running Hope. Henry has passed away and Mr Kummer has suffered a decline and willed your town to me. Please make no carefree movement and all will be well.'

He paused, smiling jovially.

'We are all friends together, *si*? I have no quarrel with anyone. If you choose to join my happy band, that is fine. There will be enough loot for all to share. If you choose to ride, now is the time to leave.'

He suddenly stopped smiling.

'Those who stay will obey my orders in everything. Is all clear?'

8

The Shy Deputy

The silence lasted, as if the whole town had gone into shock.

McQueen had thought she was past being taken by surprise, but was forced to revise her opinion; Kummer's death had been both sudden and unexpected. For a moment, she stared blankly at the Mexican.

He dressed flamboyantly in silver-trimmed clothes and gave the appearance of being no more than a fat and jolly man — but the knife in his hand, discoloured by blood, indicated his real nature.

Robbie shifted his weight from one foot to the other and McQueen said quickly, 'Stand easy, Robbie.' The big deputy relaxed.

El Tigre removed his sombrero and

made a sweeping bow. 'The señorita takes death for granted, as I do myself. I must thank you for helping the sheriff to eliminate Kummer's gunman for me. That was well done.'

His smile was back, even broader now.

'And for distracting the late Mr Kummer. You have nothing to fear from me — '

'I don't fear any man,' she said flatly.

A young cowboy hurried to the bandit's side. She recognized Pike, from the trail drive.

'It's her,' he burst out. 'The one who went for me with a knife. Crazy woman!'

El Tigre frowned. 'That is no way to speak of a lady,' he reprimanded.

McQueen said, 'This one sold out the man he worked for. He could do that again.'

The Mexican bared his teeth. 'I am aware of it, but I am not quite so trusting as your trail boss, señorita. I have explained to young Pike, as I have to each of my men, how carefully I shall disembowel him and feed him his own intestines should he attempt to betray me.'

* * *

Dusk settled a grey mantle over the quiet town of Hope. Stores were closed and only the yellow glow of oil lamps from saloon windows and a couple of horses hitched outside Doc's Place indicated life. It seemed as if the ordinary people of Hope were waiting to see if El Tigre was better or worse than the previous gang boss.

The saloon was one of the few two-storey buildings. McQueen strode inside, followed closely by Robbie. She stood a moment looking about; there was only one poker game in progress and she walked across and scrutinized faces. No Solo.

So where was he? Hiding out somewhere? If so, someone must know where.

Of course, it was midweek and the town wouldn't liven up till the ranch-hands rode in on Saturday. She noticed a blonde woman watching her and wondered if she knew something.

'Can I help you?' boomed a loud voice, and McQueen turned to face a small man with a bald head, neatly dressed in a dark suit.

'I'm Doc Pomeroy and I own this saloon. Seems to me you might be looking for a particular someone. Am I right?'

Robbie said, 'Doc's OK.'

McQueen nodded. 'Guess it's no secret,' she admitted. 'I'm hunting a man with red hair, calls himself Solo. I heard he played poker in town.'

'That's right,' Doc agreed. 'I remember him well, but he ain't here now. Guess he must have moved on. In fact, I seem to recall him aboard a horse and riding out of town not so long ago. Heading north, I fancy.'

'That so?' McQueen wasn't impressed. It was more likely he didn't want trouble and risk busting up his saloon. 'Heard someone just like you one time, Doc. A medicine show hustler.'

Doc smiled blandly at the implication he was a liar. 'Got a nice line in Women's Remedies. You want the best, I've got what you need . . . come to think of it, the one I saw was dressed all in black and carried a Bible.'

Preacher! 'Obliged to yuh, Doc, but it's the other one I'm after right this minute.'

She noticed the not-so-young blonde listening and glanced towards her. 'Know something, do you? Know where I can find him?'

'I know them all. Especially Robbie.' The blonde's laughter held mockery. 'Real bashful, ain't he?'

McQueen frowned at the big deputy. His face was red as a sunset and his feet shifted, backing away across the sawdust floor.

Another saloon girl joined in. 'Bet you don't get anywhere with Robbie. He's hopeless.'

He might have turned and fled the saloon, but a man standing at the bar laughed. Robbie paused.

McQueen noted the man had a half-filled glass in his hand and one foot on the brass rail. He might be one of El Tigre's men. Did it matter? Robbie might be bashful with women but he didn't have to put up with any man laughing at him.

Doc Pomeroy said quickly, 'No trouble in here, please. Settle any differences outside.'

The man at the bar leered at her. 'You can do better than that no-account deputy. If you want a real man, I'm willing.'

McQueen brought up her rifle, pointing it at him. Her voice held the chill of an ice-house.

'No need for trouble, Doc. Robbie, shake hands with your funny friend.'

Robbie moved forward obediently and took the man's hand, the one holding the glass in his own massive paw and squeezed. Glass shattered.

Alcohol and blood dripped into the sawdust. Bones cracked. The man screamed, tried to break away and knocked over a spittoon.

'Enough, Robbie,' she said. 'He won't feel like laughing for a while. You don't need to let any saloon woman worry you. Just ignore them — if you don't show it hurts, they'll soon quit.'

Embarrassed, Robbie nodded shyly and hurried outside.

McQueen looked around for the blonde, but Lizzie was retreating upstairs with a customer. She considered following to question her, but decided against it. The blonde might not be co-operative if she lost money.

Someone was helping the man with the crushed hand.

Doc Pomeroy approached and McQueen said, 'Your blonde knows something, that's obvious. You say you don't want trouble, so tell me what she knows. Has she got Solo tucked away somewhere?'

Doc's voice boomed. 'This redhead

you're after means nothing to me. He has a business arrangement with Liz. She's got a shack outside town — I'm not saying he's there, but he might be.'

McQueen nodded. 'Better warn Lizzie he's a killer.'

She wondered about her next move, and decided to wait for Saturday evening. Outside, on Broadway, she looked for Robbie, but he'd disappeared. She shrugged; she wasn't his keeper. She thought about Preacher, still headed north.

★ ★ ★

'No!' Amy said. 'I declare you don't seem to have the common sense you were born with. That young lady saved your life once — you can't expect her to save you next time. You must think about retiring — you're getting too old for this nonsense.'

They argued in the kitchen. Amy was rolling pastry for a pie and the sheriff chopping apples to go in it. He'd heard similar words before.

'This Mexican isn't some top gun-slinger like Henry.'

'You don't know that. Anyway, he did everyone a favour by getting rid of that Kummer person.'

'Murdered him in cold blood. Stabbed him in the back. I ought to — '

Amy banged her rolling pin down hard. 'You ought to remember you're a married man and not go tiger hunting. Besides, he's got a whole gang with him.'

'I've got Robbie.'

'Robbie's looking after the young lady.'

Baldwin snorted derision. 'You mean, she's looking after him! Some match-maker you are.' He threw out a rotten apple. 'It's my job to arrest that Mexican for murder and throw him in jail.'

Amy pounded her pastry in exasperation. 'Be realistic, Bert. He killed Kummer and one day someone will kill him. Leave well alone. Let the scum kill each other off.'

'You're forgetting I represent the law — '

'I often wish you'd forget it! You've let this law business go to your head, Bert. Your first job is to stay alive and provide for me. After that you can play at being lawman.'

'Play at — !'

Baldwin put down his knife and stalked outside. He needed a smoke. Sometimes Amy went too far.

★   ★   ★

Preacher was riding alongside the railroad track that wound between the hills. The sun was burning hot and his horse moved slowly as he pondered different plans, rejecting one after another. He was looking for a suitable site for a hold-up; and coming to the conclusion that a railroad robbery was not a job for one man alone.

His parents had been fundamentalists, and extreme with it; they had also been poor and often hungry. Preacher had stolen food from neighbours and, when nothing happened, lost his faith in a providence that did not provide.

From stealing food he graduated to stealing money and left home to support himself without working. One day, as his voice was deepening, he learned at a tented revivalist meeting how easy it was to collect from true believers. He borrowed the rantings of his father who had dealt at length with the rewards of the sinful, and his faith blossomed; at least, when a solid sermon produced a solid collection.

He continued happily until he killed his first man; a husband who objected when he found Preacher in bed with his wife. The husband, unfortunately, had been a man of some importance, so he'd changed his name to serve in the army. Now he equated religion with money, and fought the good fight to strengthen his faith.

He rounded a bend hidden by trees and saw he wasn't alone in his ambition to become rich by robbing a train. Several rough-looking *hombres* were engaged in withdrawing iron spikes and taking up the rails.

He reined back, watching them critically. Then he urged his horse forward and said, 'That's not a good idea.'

Men turned quickly, reaching for guns. 'A goddamn preacher!'

Their leader stepped forward, revolver covering the Preacher, an ugly expression on his stubble-covered face.

'Who the hell are you to say it ain't? You wanting to meet your Maker sudden-like?'

'If you succeed in robbing a train, a posse will hunt you. How long they hunt you depends on how big a haul you get. The more money, the longer they'll keep at it. Posses are human; they get discouraged and give up in time.'

Preacher spoke calmly as he looked the gang over.

'But if you wreck a train and

passengers are killed, no posse will be allowed to give up. You'll never stop running long enough to enjoy your loot.'

Some of the men were obviously impressed by his speech, but the gang leader only scowled. 'You got a better idea?'

Preacher smiled pleasantly. 'Let's see what the good book has to say.'

He opened his Bible and scooped up a revolver from a hollowed-out section. He aimed and squeezed the trigger and the gang leader went over backwards, bleeding from a third eye.

His men were too stunned to react quickly, and Preacher said confidently, 'Now we'll do the job properly. My way.'

'You killed him,' one man said, as if not believing his own words.

'May the good Lord have mercy on the soul of this sinner.'

Another of the gang asked, 'What's your way?'

'First, put back the rails so a train

can run safely over this section of the track.'

The men hesitated only briefly, then did as he ordered. Preacher reloaded his gun and put it carefully back inside his Bible. He checked the track was properly in place and said, 'Get this body out of sight.'

A couple of men dragged their original leader away and dumped him in a stand of trees.

Preacher sat his horse, surveying his new outfit. 'One of you, I hope, has a working knowledge of how railroads carry bullion?'

'Me,' a man grunted. 'Used to work for New Pacific. Got a mate who still works there.'

'And, for a cut of the proceeds, he'll provide dates and times when a train is carrying gold coin?'

''Course 'e will.'

Preacher nodded thoughtfully. 'An engine stops for coal. It stops for water. It slows when going up a gradient. It will stop at a tunnel if someone shows a red lamp. We don't need to risk killing women and children to stop a train and get some posse mad at us.'

He looked them over, satisfied; his years of preaching experience had taught him how to hypnotize an audience with words.

'I've got a hideout no one knows about. There's a river we can use to lose our trail — '

'A bullion train will have an armed guard.'

The speaker was the man with a friend in New Pacific, and Preacher studied him carefully. He was older than most of the gang and looked stolid and calm; he was the only one who hadn't drawn a gun when Preacher first showed himself.

'What's your name?'

'Ned.'

'Well, Ned, you're an important man in my eyes, so when I'm not around, you're in charge. Guards are paid to risk their lives. If possible, we won't harm them but if we have to shoot them, the Lord will understand our need. But we don't touch passengers.'

'Makes sense,' one of the gang murmured, and the others agreed.

Preacher allowed himself a small smile, knowing he had them in his hand.

9

Double Cross Brand

McQueen sat with Robbie just inside the blacksmith's shop next door to the livery stable. They sat in cool shadow watching the smith reshoe Nemesis.

The smith was nowhere near as big as Robbie, but he had well-developed muscles and a knack with a hammer and tongs as he shaped red-hot iron on his anvil. There was a smell of burning hair.

He didn't even look up as Cousin Jack and young Pike walked in. Jack said, 'We're from El Tigre. Come to collect his ten per cent, same as you paid Kummer.'

The smith glanced at them, unspeaking, and continued his work. Nemesis stood patiently as he nailed a shoe to a hoof.

111

Then Jack recognized the big horse. 'That black stallion was my cousin's. How did you get it? Guess it's mine now.'

The smith's white teeth flashed in his smoke-grimed face. 'See McQueen about that. She rode him here.'

Pike grinned. 'McQueen! That crazy . . . she only had a mule when I saw her. Take what's yours, Jack.'

Robbie stood up silently, looming like some dark giant in the firelight. His voice rumbled, 'No.'

Jack heard the click of a rifle being cocked, and turned to see McQueen covering them both with her rifle.

She said quietly, 'You're a fool, Pike, and fools don't last long. Wade will hang you when he catches up. That's if El Tigre doesn't open you up with his knife first. You don't have a future, especially not as a trouble maker.'

She inspected the other man with a calculating eye.

'Jack, you look like a man who's been around and learned what's what. I found this black on the open range and, as far as I'm concerned, it's finders keepers. The horse is mine.'

Pike retreated hurriedly, his face pale and his lips compressed.

Jack gave a tight little smile. 'We'll see what El Tigre says about that.'

He walked out, with Pike following. The young ex-cowboy asked, 'D'yuh know where Tigre is?'

'He mentioned the Emporium.' Jack turned along the boardwalk to the store, where El Tigre, all smiles, was talking with the owner, a tall thin man who looked unimpressed.

'Of course, you will get more in return for the tax you pay, Señor Howard. Besides my personal protection, I have plans to develop this town. Too many have left because of that cheapskate Kummer.' The Mexican shook his head sadly. 'So short-sighted.'

His voice became smooth as oil. 'I want to see people coming here to settle, to farm, to open mines. I want,

113

like you, *señor*, to see Hope grow into a boom town.'

He cut himself a piece of cheese, helped himself to a cracker from the barrel and munched contentedly.

'I have a plan. Together, we shall nominate this town for state capital and promote it — I have connections with a railroad company you see — and then the folk with money will flock here and we'll all get rich. Why, if the number of residents doubles, I could halve the tax you pay me!'

His swarthy face beamed in approval of his own generosity.

'We shall need a town council, of course, and I suggest myself for mayor. You, Señor Howard, shall be a councilman. And Pomeroy, he too seems a suitable candidate.

'But enough dreaming . . . you have a problem, Jack?'

'My cousin's horse — McQueen claims it's hers. I want — '

El Tigre frowned. 'Jack, please, do not stir trouble. The lady boards with

114

the sheriff and that big deputy goes around with her. Leave her be. McQueen interests me, so leave her alone — I intend to keep an eye on her myself.'

★　★　★

McQueen and Robbie watched the men of Double Cross ranch ride into town on Saturday evening. They had chairs in the sheriff's office, with the door wide open. Robbie's was almost solid wood to take his weight.

The cowhands arrived at the gallop, dressed in their best, with wild whoops and shooting revolvers into the air; they'd got their pay and wanted liquor and saloon women. They swaggered along boardwalks and El Tigre's men kept out of the way. So did the sheriff.

If the cowboys noticed the change of ownership, they didn't let it inhibit them. This was a time for fun, for letting their hair down. They had no interest in who ran Hope.

Gathering darkness made identifying faces difficult. Solo might already have arrived. The sky was cloudy and the glow of oil lamps tended to change the colour of hair.

McQueen said, 'Come on,' left her chair and Robbie followed her past the barber's and a couple of empty shops. She led the way down an alley between the billiard hall and Doc's Place. They waited in shadow.

Presently a horseman rode in, avoiding lighted areas. He walked his horse up the alley and hitched to a post behind the saloon. A back door opened and the man entered. The door closed.

McQueen waited a few minutes, then moved quietly around to a side window. Several card games were in progress and, at one table, was a face she recognized — or was almost sure she did. Solo. But this man had muddy brown hair. She frowned.

'You want me to get him?' Robbie asked.

She didn't doubt he could; but he

also made a big target. She wanted to get the card player to herself in a good light so she could be sure.

In the saloon, the noise level was rising; music played, dancers gyrated, men laughed. The blonde would know; but Solo wouldn't care what happened to her.

McQueen hesitated in breaking up a card game played by cowhands who were armed and drinking freely.

'No, Robbie, leave him for the moment. I want to get him outside, alone. Take a look at his face so you'll know him.'

She remembered the horse hitched at the rear of the building and went to take a look. As far as she could tell, the animal was a regular cowpony; a mare.

She studied the horse, getting the first glimmer of an idea, when an amused voice drawled, 'You are, perhaps, considering entering the horse-stealing business, *señorita*? Perhaps you wish to join my band of outlaws?'

El Tigre eased his fat body out of the

shadows, smiling pleasantly.

'I tell my men to behave themselves while the cowboys are in town — and here is the young lady who boards with the law acting suspiciously.'

McQueen said, 'Robbie, watch the front of the building. I don't want Solo to just walk away from us.'

She looked coolly at El Tigre. A half-formed plan rapidly took shape; she calculated the Mexican was the man she wanted for this job.

'Think you could put a Double Cross brand on this mare? So it would look like an old brand?'

El Tigre threw back his head and laughed. 'You are the most surprising young lady. But, of course; I can perform that simple task with little trouble. Changing a brand is something I learned as a *chico* — at my father's knee, *si?*'

She nodded.

'But not here in this alley, *señorita*. We lead the horse to the smithy where I shall perform this small service. I trust you will not be reporting this to your sheriff?'

'That's not what I have in mind.'

'Intriguing, but it shall be as you say.'

He unhitched the mare and led her confidently out of the alley and along Broadway. McQueen followed. Solo would be playing for hours, the cowboys drinking. Her plan should work . . .

* * *

Big Robbie stood in a doorway across Broadway, watching the front entrance of Doc's Place. He observed how steadily men walked in, and unsteadily out. He looked for the man who'd once had red hair, but now had brown. The change of colour confused him, but he felt sure he'd know the face, and he could remember the name: Solo.

Along the street, stores and houses were quiet, with few lights showing; only the saloons were doing any business. Cowboys continued to ride in and hitch their mounts; some he knew from the past when he'd patrolled Broadway with the sheriff. Since Kummer had taken over, Bert stayed home.

But Kummer was dead and still Bert didn't patrol. Robbie wished his head didn't ache when he tried to puzzle things out. He wished he were like other men who seemed to understand these things quickly. His lady was quick to understand too.

Presently he saw her come out of the alley with El Tigre and a horse, and watched them walk together in the direction of the livery stable.

Robbie scowled. He didn't like her being with a Mexican. He got an unpleasant feeling when he saw them together but didn't understand why; someone else might have told him he was jealous.

What could a greaser do that he couldn't? Why hadn't she asked him? He almost went after her to tell her that.

Then he remembered he was supposed to watch to see that Solo didn't come out the front way, and shook his head. Luckily he'd remembered in time. The lady thought it important and that was the job she'd given him. He settled down to wait.

* * *

The livery stable was closed and dark but El Tigre opened up the smithy as easily as if he'd got a key to the place. He lit a fire and used bellows to encourage it.

He went to the door and whistled, and a small man appeared, grey-haired and bandy-legged.

'Angelo, a branding job.' The small man vanished and returned in a few minutes with a long iron.

El Tigre put it in the fire to heat. To McQueen, he said, 'Angelo is my expert with horses.'

She watched Angelo remove the saddle from Solo's horse, quietly talking all the time and stroking the mare. He persuaded her to kneel for him, then rolled her on to one side. He brought pigging strings from a shirt pocket and hobbled her front legs, then the rear. The horse lay still, watching him, listening.

El Tigre selected a blanket, thin with age. and dampened it. When he was satisfied with both the blanket and the hot iron, he laid the blanket against the mare to brand her through it.

He printed two separate slashes, then reversed the iron and made two more slashes on top of the first two to give a double cross. He removed the blanket and inspected his work.

'*Sí*, that should do.'

McQueen looked closely; the brand was plain enough to see if you looked for it, but apparently faint with age. It would pass a casual inspection by a drunken cowboy in poor light.

'It will do, *señorita*?'

'It'll do fine.'

'I must admit I am intrigued . . . '

'Stick around, at a safe distance, and you'll see something.'

Angelo freed the mare and she came to her feet, shaking herself. He saddled her, and McQueen led her around the back of Doc's Place and hitched her to the post.

Robbie joined her. 'Solo's still playing cards. What yuh doing?'

'Baiting a lure to bring him out.'

They waited in shadow till a cowhand the worse for drink visited the outhouse. On his return, McQueen pointed to Solo's mare.

'Can you read a brand for me?'

'You interested in brands, ma'am? Let me see — '

He bent over, swaying, squinting, then sobered up. 'That's Double Cross. Did yuh see who was riding her?'

'The gambler dressed like a cowboy — the one taking all your money.'

'You sure?'

'Saw him ride into town on her.'

Before McQueen could stop him, the cowhand staggered through the doorway into the saloon, shouting, 'Double Cross horse-thief!'

10

A Hanging Matter

McQueen swore in an unladylike manner. She'd intended to lure Solo outside, not alert a bunch of liquored-up cowhands with the cry of 'horse-thief!'

In the sudden hush, she said, 'Damn, damn, damn,' and turned to Robbie beside her. 'Better get the sheriff here.'

The big deputy hesitated, and she gave him a push. 'Now!'

A slurred voice from inside the saloon said, 'Where, Olly?'

'Right here — our new gambling friend. Not satisfied with taking our money, he lifts our horseflesh too.'

A voice she remembered well said, impatiently, 'Shut up and play cards if you're not too drunk.'

'I'm not too drunk to know a

horse-thief when I see one.'

'That's a hanging matter,' another cowhand added.

'You crazy? My horse doesn't carry your brand.'

'Step outside and prove it, mister.'

The doorway was suddenly crowded with men holding revolvers pointed at Solo. McQueen stepped back hurriedly, into the shadows.

Surrounded by cowboys, Solo pointed at the mare. 'That's my horse.'

Two or three men bent to inspect the brand. 'Double Cross plain enough.'

'Jeez, you *hombres* are plain loco,' Solo said in a disgusted tone. 'Let me show yuh.'

He pushed his way forward to the mare and looked for himself. 'How — ? I've not seen this brand before.'

Someone laughed. 'You'd better have a real good explanation, fellar.'

Solo didn't have any kind of explanation. It was his horse — but the brand was Double Cross. He was mystified. 'I don't understand — '

'Enough,' a man said curtly. 'Get a rope. String the thieving bastard up.'

Solo reached for his Colt, too late. Someone brought a gun barrel down on his wrist, cracking it. His revolver clattered on the ground. Desperate, he tried to run; hands held him. He kicked out. A blow to his head half-stunned him. He was hustled on to Broadway by an angry crowd of Double Cross men.

The clouds had cleared and the moon shone brightly. McQueen could see beyond any doubt that she'd found her man, even if his hair had been dyed. She imagined Lizzie was responsible for that. The face was the familiar one from her nightmare.

Solo was dragged along to the Three Star Emporium. The store had a hoist for unloading, and a rope was cast up and over this. A cowpuncher borrowed a horse and cart and manoeuvred it under the hoist. Solo, pale and looking sick, and still protesting his innocence, was lifted on to the wagon, hands tied behind his back.

She saw Robbie and Sheriff Baldwin hurrying along the boardwalk, but it was obvious they were not going to be in time to prevent a lynching.

A noose went around Solo's neck and pulled tight and the other end made fast.

Baldwin shouted, 'Don't do it!'

Solo croaked, 'No . . . no . . . '

A cowboy quirted the horse and it started forward. Wagon wheels rolled and Solo's feet dangled in the air, toes reaching desperately for something, anything solid. His head jerked sideways as his weight came on the knot in the rope; he hung suspended, choking, legs kicking, tongue showing and eyes bulging. His body twisted as it hung there, suspended by a broken neck.

McQueen stood rigid, feeling no elation. She felt dry, as if dust clogged her throat. Again she had been cheated of her revenge.

She saw bald-headed Doc Pomeroy watching her from the doorway of his saloon, his face expressionless. El Tigre was another interested spectator, a tight smile on his face. Cowhands began to drift away as Baldwin arrived, looking grim.

'Cut him down, Robbie.'

McQueen said, 'Don't let it bother yuh, Sheriff. He got what he deserved.'

The sheriff looked angry. 'Who d'yuh think you are to decide that? I don't want Judge Lynch in my town — that's not how the law works.'

McQueen shrugged. 'Guess I'll be moving on in the morning.'

As she walked away, El Tigre murmured, 'I admire that *señorita*. We have more in common than you think.'

She compressed her lips. It was a thought that didn't make her happy.

* * *

McQueen was up early in the morning. She got her things together and was about to leave the house when the sheriff's wife appeared in her nightgown.

'You'll have breakfast before you go,' Amy said firmly urging her into the kitchen. 'It won't take but a moment to reliven the stove and boil coffee and get something hot inside you. Sit down.'

McQueen dumped her bedroll and sat; watching Amy bustle about, she thought she seemed another woman with her hair down.

'You don't have to leave on account of Bert getting upset last night. I'm always telling him he takes his lawing too seriously.'

'It's not that,' McQueen said. 'I've got another job elsewhere.'

'Well, I ain't criticizing. You saved my man's life and that puts you on the side of the angels as far as I'm concerned, but it does appear you're a mite hard for your own good. Robbie, now, he likes yuh — and you've been good for him.'

McQueen shrugged. 'I guess Robbie's all right, for a man.'

'Eat up now.' Amy put a plate filled with bacon and hash in front of her and

129

sat, nursing a mug of coffee. McQueen suddenly found she was hungry and cleaned the plate and accepted coffee.

'That's better,' Amy said, smiling. 'One last thing, I want you to have this. I think it'll help you — '

She reached into a sideboard and brought out a book bound in black cloth. A Bible.

McQueen reacted violently. She felt the blood drain from her face; her hand shook, spilling coffee. She dropped the mug and pushed her chair back, recoiling. 'No!'

Amy stared in amazement.

McQueen shuddered, reliving her nightmare. The Preacher. The Bible that changed into a gun. Her mother screaming as her father's body jerked each time a bullet went home, dying before her eyes.

'No!' There was horror in her voice. She grabbed her bedroll and rifle and rushed outside. Broadway was almost deserted. She ran to the livery stable and began to saddle Nemesis with trembling fingers. The stallion seemed glad to see her.

★ ★ ★

Robbie usually got up as dawn woke the horses in the stable where he slept. He put his head under the pump, brushed hay off his clothes and went for breakfast at the café. Normally he would wait at the Sheriff's Office for his orders; but since Amy had insisted he protect the lady, he hadn't bothered.

This morning he shivered with apprehension, remembering McQueen had said she'd be moving on. The idea of losing her filled him with a sense of panic. What could he do? He'd been lonely before, and didn't want to go back to that.

No one had ever explained things like the lady did. Bert got impatient with him. She didn't make fun of him the way the saloon women did. He got on well with Nemesis; the big stallion wouldn't let just anyone feed him slices of apple.

He didn't want the lady to leave. He wasn't sure what he did want, but not that. Returning from the café, he found her saddling up.

'You're going away? Leaving now?'

She seemed surprised to see him; perhaps she didn't realize he slept at the stable?

'Yes, Robbie.' She was upset about something, he could tell, and fighting for calm.

He stroked Nemesis. 'Nice horse.'

'It's time for me to take the trail.'

'Wish I was going,' he said desperately. 'You don't laugh at me. You're the only one ever to take me seriously. Can't I go with you?'

She hesitated. Would the sheriff blame Robbie for the lynching? 'I'm hunting a man, one I'm going to kill.'

'Like Solo? A bad man?'

She hesitated again. Keep it simple. 'Yes, like him.'

'I could help. I'd do anything you say.

Let me come with you. Please.'

Finally, after looking at him a long time, she said, 'All right. Have you got a horse?'

'A mule. I'll get my stuff.'

Excited, he packed his saddle-bags, dug the money he'd saved from its hiding place, and gave his deputy's badge to the hostler to return. He saddled the mule.

Robbie felt like singing. He was going to see the world with his new friend. Excitement bubbled. He was starting a new life.

'Ready, lady, I'm ready.'

She said, 'As we're travelling together, I've got a name. You call me Jo.'

'Jo,' he repeated.

Half an hour later they were riding north, leaving Hope behind.

★   ★   ★

'I don't fancy being a mule driver,' Curly said.

The Preacher smiled a tight smile. 'I don't imagine yuh do. You fancy yourself a gunslick — that's why you're staying with the mules. I don't want anyone spraying lead around when there's no need.'

Curly, the youngest in the gang, wore his Colt .45 in a tied-down holster; he spent a lot of time practising a quick draw. Preacher considered him too hot-headed to be allowed near passengers.

'Later, if we're facing a posse, you can throw all the lead that's necessary. For this hold-up I don't want any shooting — take the coin, load it on to our mules, and travel.'

They were waiting, with their horses and a mule train, among a clump of trees near a water tank; bushes screened them from view and a leafy canopy provided shade. They waited for the bullion coach Ned's informer had promised.

'Don't see why we need mules at all.'

'Because the coin comes in ammunition boxes, and they're heavy.'

Curly grunted, and another man asked, 'Suppose a passenger shows himself?'

'One bullet over his head and he'll dive back in the carriage like the Devil in person was after him.'

Ned had been listening to the rails. 'Train coming,' he said.

'Quiet now, and keep out of sight until after it stops. Ned, you handle the engineer and fireman. Who's got the dynamite?'

'Me,' a lanky man drawled.

'Stay close by me. We'll open up the express car the easy way.'

'Now, Curly, listen carefully. Once the door is open, bring up the mules and be ready to load. And I don't want to see a gun in your hand. Is that clear?'

'Yeah, yeah,' Curly said sullenly.

They waited, only the Preacher relaxed, calm and confident. The iron rails vibrated as the train approached. Brakes squealed and couplings rattled. Steam hissed. The train slowed right down and eased along to the tank and stopped.

Preacher adjusted his mask and raised his Bible in the air. He saw the fireman step down to unhook the hosepipe and brought his arm down.

Masked riders surged out from the trees with guns in their hands. Ned pointed his rifle at the engineer.

'Step this way, fellar. We don't want yuh starting off just yet.'

The engineer looked sour-faced and hesitated before climbing from the cab. 'You're wasting your time,' he growled. 'There's armed guards aboard this train.'

Preacher dismounted, put away his Bible and advanced towards the express car with a stick of dynamite in his hand. He looked over the door of the car and decided on the projecting handle.

'Another,' he told the lanky man.

He tied two sticks of dynamite to the handle with cord and lit a cheroot. He puffed on it till the tip glowed red in the breeze, then lit both fuses and calmly walked back a few yards.

Two short sharp explosions merged

as one and the car door disintegrated.

He walked forward and peered inside; the two guards were dazed, with blood trickling from noses and ears.

'Throw down your guns, gents, and no one need be hurt.'

'You bastard — goddamn you to hell!'

Preacher back-handed him across the mouth. 'Don't take the name of the Lord in vain.'

Other members of the gang hurried up, and Curly brought the mules.

'One box each side of a mule, for balance,' the Preacher directed.

Somewhere along the train, a passenger looked out of a carriage window and called, 'What's going on?'

A masked man sent a bullet close to his head and he withdrew hurriedly.

Preacher walked up and down, keeping an eye on everything. 'Tighten that strap. Get the mules moving. Go.'

He swung on to his horse and rode up to the locomotive. 'Job's finished,' he told Ned. 'Let's ride.'

137

He turned to the engineer. 'You may continue your journey when ready.'

'Thanks for nothing!'

Preacher followed the mules, watching over the ammunition boxes. Even Curly was happier now. They reached shallow water and followed the river upstream. Preacher led them on to stony ground and up to the abandoned fort in the hills.

11

At the Junction

Commissioner Lewis sat at his desk shuffling paperwork; sometimes he wondered why he'd accepted the job. The door was open and his coat off. His expression was glum.

Since the rail hold-up there was nothing but bad news. The railroad wanted an immediate arrest. His superior wanted action. He simply had not enough men to please everyone; there were already too many thieves and murderers roaming his territory. No matter how he juggled his marshals there were not enough men to cope with all the calls for help that arrived at his office. US marshals were in short supply.

When he'd first learned of the train robbery he'd used the telegraph to reach Yates, at the next stop on his route, and redirected him to Crow Junction to investigate. It was especially worrying because this gang seemed to have a leader with more than half a brain.

Lewis had quit smoking years ago but, right now, he wished he hadn't. He could use a drink, and looked at the clock. He really should wait until . . .

A telegraph messenger hurried through the doorway. 'Your office is sure keeping us busy, Mr Lewis.'

Lewis held out his hand for the form. Inwardly he was cursing the railroad and the telegraph company. In the old days bad news travelled slowly and a man had time to get his thinking done.

Then he sat up straight as he read this new telegraph from the sheriff at Crow Junction:

Leader of hold-up gang said to be preacher wearing a black coat and carrying a Bible.

Preacher! Lewis cursed as he thought of Jo. She needed to be told; but

Preacher would now have armed men around him. He wouldn't be easy to get at.

Lewis could remember a time when he, too, had faced a gang of robbers; he'd got their leader, but he'd taken a bullet in the leg. The doctor had saved his leg but he used a cane to cover up his limp. And the old wound still hurt when it rained. He didn't want that for Jo.

Hell and damnation! He'd have to go himself. He remembered Bill Wade should be at Crow, selling his herd, and scribbled a note on a blank and handed it to the waiting messenger.

'Get this away pronto.'

Bill would warn Jo. Meanwhile he had to travel. At least he'd get there fast — by rail — and, if they wanted him to chase their robbers, for free. He always had a travelling bag packed ready and the next train didn't leave for an hour. Time for a quick drink.

★ ★ ★

141

It turned into a slow journey, slow because of Robbie's mule, but McQueen was in no hurry.

His mule was a big one but, even so, Robbie's feet almost touched the ground when he was in the saddle. And he carried a lot of weight.

Nemesis settled into a leisurely pace; the big stallion seemed happy to oblige the big man. McQueen wondered how much this was due to Robbie sleeping in the same stable. Or perhaps it was his quiet singing that moved easily from one sentimental ballad to another as they travelled. He had a knack with animals even if he was scared of women. McQueen found herself relaxing.

When they rode into Crow Junction, past the yards and cattle pens, it appeared the railhead was indulging in a frenzy of excitement. Armed horsemen were forming up with a sheriff at their head; a posse was about to ride out.

McQueen wasn't interested. She headed towards the trestle bridge over a creek, the water low, and the depot. There was always a hotel near a railroad depot.

The town looked much the same as any Western town, a line of saloons and stores and shacks; this one was bigger than most because the rails stopped here and cattlemen shipped their herds east.

They walked their mounts along Main Street till Robbie said, 'Eats,' and pointed to a shop front labelled *Dining Rooms*.

She had learned that a man his size needed a large intake. 'Sure, we'll eat first.'

They dismounted, hitched their animals and went inside. With most men apparently heading out of town, the place was almost empty. Two men sat at the back, talking quietly over their meal.

McQueen stopped and stared. Bill Wade she could understand; he had cattle to sell. But he was seated opposite her Uncle Lew.

Neither seemed surprised to see her, but both regarded Robbie with more than casual interest. 'Who's your big friend?' Lew asked.

'This is Robbie. Robbie, meet my Uncle Lew. And Bill Wade, a trail boss I worked for.'

Wade smiled. 'Sure did, and I've sold my cattle and got pay for yuh.'

'You didn't hire me, Mr Wade. I was just dumped on yuh.'

Lew frowned. 'Never turn away honest money, Jo. It's being broke tempts some folk into dishonest ways.'

'Besides which, you earned it,' Wade said.

McQueen looked hard at her uncle. 'What are you doing here anyway? I thought you agreed to let me handle it on my own.'

'I did, and I'm going to. The situation has got a little more complicated since we last met.'

Wade said, 'First, sit down and order — I can see Robbie's wasting away.'

Robbie beamed at his new friends,

144

'Steak, lots of steak.'

'It does a cattleman good to hear those words.'

The food came promptly and they ate, Robbie with enthusiasm and McQueen sparingly.

Lew said casually, 'I heard Fletch was taken care of. Since you're here, I assume Solo is no longer with us?'

'That's right.' She gave a brief account of what had happened.

Lew commented, 'Dead's dead. El Tigre sounds like a job for one of my marshals, when I've got one to spare. Or a younger sheriff. More likely, Hope will just fade away as more people up and leave.'

'And young Pike's there? Wa'al, I guess he won't last long,' Wade said. 'I'll leave him for this Mexican to deal with.'

'There's news of Preacher?' McQueen asked.

'The reason I'm here,' Lew said, 'is because there's been a train robbery. It seems a small time gang have got themselves a new boss with big ideas. The railroad's screaming for blood ... and one rumour describes the leader of the hold-up gang as a red-haired man wearing black and holding a Bible.'

'*Preacher!*'

'It seems likely,' Lew admitted. 'The railroad President is hopping mad and offering a reward of one thousand dollars. With a price on his head, you're going to have competition from bounty hunters.'

McQueen scowled. 'So? They're only after money while I've got a personal score to settle. Any bounty hunter who gets in my way will wish he hadn't. Where d'yuh reckon this gang is now?'

Lew spread his hands. 'Plenty of hiding places in the hills. I'm not betting that posse will find anything much. I've got one marshal looking, fellar named Yates. He spotted Solo for yuh, so you might say 'thanks' if you run across him.'

McQueen nodded curtly and stood

up. 'I'll be riding then.'

Lew shook his head. 'Leave it till morning, Jo, There may be news. I'll book you a room at the Drovers' Hotel.' He looked at Robbie. 'Not sure about your friend though — reckon they've only got ordinary-sized beds.'

Robbie beamed. 'I usually bed down with the horses.'

'Makes sense. Take good care of Jo.'

'I'll do that, sir.'

McQueen paused, then spoke to the trail boss. 'Is Chester here?'

'No. Chester and the rest of the crew have gone back. I only stayed on because Lew let me know he was coming.'

McQueen moved towards the door. 'Yeah, well, I'll wait till morning. Then I aim to comb those hills.'

Lew waved his cane. 'Just remember that Preacher has a gang with him now.'

* * *

Preacher, with Ned, took a roundabout route to Crow Junction, approaching

147

from a direction opposite to the hideout. He saw nothing of the posse, but heard a drumming of hoofs far off.

The night was cloudy with intermittent starlight, and Preacher let Ned find the way.

'Ain't you taking a chance, dressed that way with bright red hair?'

He smiled. 'First, no one will be expecting me to ride openly into town. Second, out of any direct light my hair appears dark. Third, I'll keep my hat on.'

Their horses moved along slowly, quietly, as they neared the depot, Ned carrying a heavy canvas bag. The rails gleamed and locomotive sheds made dark bulky shapes in the gloom.

'You really aiming to hit another train soon?'

'The sooner the better — the authorities won't be expecting that. Is your friend reliable?'

'Sure, he hates the railroad — as long as he gets his share you can rely on him . . . we're here.'

They walked their horses into deep shadow and hitched behind the depot. Preacher heard drunken singing and laughter from the saloons on Main Street.

Ned tapped on a wooden door and whispered, 'Dan, it's me.'

The door opened a fraction, showing a faint glimmer of oil light. Ned pushed it wider and slid inside, and Preacher followed. The railroad man shut the door and turned up the lamp; the windows were covered by thick curtains.

The railroad man stared at him. 'You've got a nerve coming into town.'

Preacher smiled. 'The Lord is my strength and salvation. There is nothing to fear.'

Ned said, 'Dan, this is our new boss. Preach, this here gent is Daniels, mostly called Dan.'

The Preacher removed his hat and sat down. 'Ned, the bag. Man does not live by bread alone.'

Daniels, he noted, had a twisted arm and seemed in some pain; his thin face was pinched.

Ned hefted the canvas bag on to the table and opened it; a shower of gold coins spilled out.

'That's more like it,' Dan said.

'I should warn you against reckless spending — '

'I'm not a fool. Now. I was surely a damned fool ever to work for the railroad. After my accident, they refused to pay any compensation, or pension. I'm supposed to survive on a low-paid clerking job' — his voice was bitter — 'and pretend I'm grateful. This goes towards my secret pension fund.'

'There will be more,' Preacher said confidently. 'The Lord will provide.'

'Well, Preach, let me tell you a few things, so you'll be careful too. There's a US marshal in town asking questions, and I've just heard the railroad has gone to Pinkerton to hire a detective. They have a reputation, you know — '

'So have I. They are due a surprise shortly, if you can tell me the date and timing of the next train to carry coin.'

Daniels stared. 'That takes some gall.'

'They won't be expecting us so soon after the last hold-up . . . and next time we'll strike elsewhere.'

Daniels laughed his brittle laugh. 'I like that. Here's the schedule . . .'

★ ★ ★

McQueen, riding Nemesis, set out with Robbie, on his mule at first light, following the rail track back to the water tank.

The posse had returned, without news of the robbers. There had been no word from Yates.

From the tank, the tracks were obvious; horses and mules had travelled together and were easy to follow till they reached the river.

'Which way now?' Robbie asked.

'Well, they sure enough left the river somewhere. Let's move up high and see if we can spot anything.'

They rode leisurely between trees,

climbing steadily towards the top of a hill and discovered a man sitting on a horse watching them. He was motionless in the shade and held a rifle covering them.

'If you're hunting train robbers, I advise turning back,' he said.

McQueen reined in, staring at him. 'Who the hell are you to give advice?'

'I'm a professional hunter of men for their reward money, and I don't want amateurs horning in.' He lifted a small telescope. 'Saw yuh miles away. You got no hope of tracking anyone without being seen.'

Robbie said, 'You've no right to stop us.'

Cold eyes appraised the big man. 'Maybe not, but a rifle bullet from cover deters most.'

McQueen held on to her temper. 'Let it lay, Robbie. Now, mister, whatever your name is — ?'

'Vince is my name. Well known in some quarters.'

'I don't doubt it.' She looked him

152

over carefully. He carried a rifle, a revolver and a Bowie knife. He wore buckskin and had long hair and a beard that came to a point.

'Listen, Vince, I want the Preacher and I aim to kill him. It's a personal thing. I don't want the rest of the gang, or their loot, or the reward money. If you let us tag along with yuh you've got help and you still get the reward.'

'Don't need help.'

Nemesis began to move restlessly and Vince smiled coldly. 'Can't even control your horse.'

Lew would know him, she thought.

'My uncle is a Commissioner of federal marshals. I can get information you can't. Robbie here is strong as a team of oxen, so think again.'

McQueen reflected, a bounty hunter was used to tracking men; he knew things a part-time posse couldn't possibly know.

She said, 'Find the Preacher and let me have one clear shot at him. That's all I'll need. I'll ride away with Robbie and you collect your money.'

Vince looked hard at her. 'You sound serious.'

'I'm serious.'

He still hesitated, then finally said, 'It's a deal. You get your shot at him.'

He slid his rifle into its scabbard and waved his hand to indicate the apparently empty hills.

'Must be a thousand hide-aways around here, but there's a short cut to our quarry — if you can find out when the next load of coin is travelling.'

'I can do that,' she said confidently, assuming Lew would know.

'Then we'll get down to the Junction and ride the train. Let the robbers come to us.'

12

Too Many Hunters

To McQueen's surprise, Vince didn't hurry. His route was circuitous, keeping to the high ground and stopping from time to time to spy out the land through his telescope.

She noticed Robbie was lagging behind and not his usual cheerful self. Vince had warned him against singing, in case it gave their position away, but she didn't think it was that. Robbie had a way of ignoring small setbacks to his routine.

His face was clouded, as if struggling with some new and troublesome idea.

She slowed Nemesis till the mule caught up. 'What is it, Robbie? Maybe I can help.'

He looked sadly at her. 'You said you were going to kill a preacher. A preacher reads from the Bible, Jo. He's a good man. Why would you want to kill one?'

McQueen was taken aback. Robbie, she realized again, took casual speech literally. Now she had to think how to explain to him.

'This one is not a real preacher in a church. It's just a name he uses. He's only pretending to be a preacher — he's really an evil man.'

The big man was indignant. 'Pretends to be a holy man — he shouldn't do that!'

He rode on again, silent, thinking. McQueen waited patiently, wondering what was coming next.

'Jo, do you have to kill him? It says in the Bible that you shouldn't kill.'

She was almost tempted to suggest he tell that to the Preacher. Instead, with a sigh, she brought from a shirt pocket the warrant and badge Lew had given her.

Robbie stared in wonder. 'A United States Marshal! You're a deputy marshal?' He was excited.

'The man who calls himself the Preacher is a wanted criminal — you know about Wanted posters, Robbie. He's a murderer and has to be stopped before he kills again.'

And that's only half of it, she thought grimly.

'Yes, yes, I understand. I was a deputy sheriff, remember, with Bert. And now I'm riding with a deputy US marshal.'

He started to sing again, until Vince reminded him to keep the noise down.

By the time they approached Crow Junction, shadows were thickening, oil lamps being lit and the saloons refilling for another nightly session of drinking and gambling.

McQueen rode with Robbie, slightly behind the bounty hunter as he headed for the livery stable. Passing a group of townsmen it soon became obvious that he was, as he claimed, well-known in some quarters.

'It's one of those bounty men. Hi, you — get outa town. You ain't wanted here.'

Vince ignored the shout and rode calmly on. But other men joined in, and some stepped into the road, crowding about his horse. A few still had whiskey glasses in their hands.

Vince reined back and sat quietly as they shouted at him.

'Blood-sucker!'

'You keep away — we don't want your kind here.'

'If there's any money going, we want it!'

McQueen was surprised; she hadn't realized bounty men were actively disliked. Perhaps some members of the posse were envious of his ability to succeed where they had failed.

A man laid his hand on the horse's reins, and Vince hit him across the head with the barrel of his revolver. 'Get away from my horse!'

As the man went down, the crowd turned ugly. 'Get him!'

Hands reached out and pulled Vince from the saddle. He, too, went down amid jeers and boots.

McQueen glanced at Robbie. 'Looks like we have to deal ourselves in.'

Robbie grinned broadly. 'Help Vince,' he said.

He stepped off his mule and picked up two men, one with each hand, and tossed them aside. He grabbed two more and cracked their heads together. Vince climbed to his feet and swung his revolver barrel. Men came from the saloons each side of Main Street to join in with wild whoops.

An Irish voice boomed 'Fight!' and more men appeared, some armed with clubs. As they waded in with fists and boots, McQueen realized that in any Western town a free-for-all was regarded as legitimate entertainment.

'Get the bounty man!'

It seemed someone hadn't forgotten what had started the fight. Robbie stood solidly alongside Vince, a mountain of a man among pygmies. Then someone climbed up his broad back with a knife in his hand.

McQueen frowned and uncoiled her

159

bull whip and sent the lash snaking out. It went around the knife-man's neck and she jerked the stock. He came off Robbie's back, half-strangled.

The fight might have gone on until someone was seriously hurt if her Uncle Lew hadn't come limping along the dusty street carrying a shotgun. He fired one barrel above the heads of the crowd and reloaded.

'Next load will scatter among yuh, and I don't care who you are. Break it up. I want this street cleared pronto.'

Fighting men began to sidle away with sheepish expressions: a shotgun had that effect.

Robbie came up, grinning. 'Good fight!'

'Yeah,' Vince agreed. 'And I'm glad you were on my side.'

Lew glowered at McQueen. 'What brought that on?'

She indicated Vince. 'Meet our new partner — he's going to lead us to Preacher.'

Lew looked at the bounty man. 'I

know you, don't I? Could be, I suppose. You all right, Jo?'

'I could eat something.'

'Yes,' Robbie added, beaming. 'More steak!'

As they headed towards the dining-rooms, Vince said, 'All we really need to know is when and where the next train carries gold coin.'

'Is that all?'

★ ★ ★

McQueen, with Robbie and Vince, rode across country to the shipping point the day before the next payout was due, and watched the heavy boxes being loaded. They led their mounts up a ramp into a cattle truck before settling into a passenger carriage.

The locomotive built a head of steam, the whistle blew and the brakes came off. Their carriage lurched into motion.

Robbie was excited. Travelling with Jo was turning out to be even better

161

than he'd imagined. He liked her Uncle Lew and the idea that a cattleman wanted him to eat more big steaks. He enjoyed taking care of the black stallion in the stable at night. He was beginning to like Vince because he could fight.

The world beyond Hope, he was finding, was full of different people and all sorts of new things, even if he didn't understand half of them.

And now a ride on a train. He was like a small boy, jumping up and down at the carriage window as the landscape rushed past. It was his first time to ride the iron rails.

'Fast,' he said, beaming. 'Much faster!'

Anticipating a hold-up somewhere along the track, McQueen held her rifle ready. Only Vince was relaxed, feet up and hat tilted across his eyes.

The wheels clattered over the track; smoke blew back in a black plume; the carriage rocked.

A man came slowly along the centre aisle, pausing to study each passenger.

He wore a grey suit and Derby hat and flat-heeled boots. His face could have graced a bulldog.

He passed on and, presently, returned. He stopped to stare at Vince, then knocked the hat away the better to see his face.

'Don't I know you, fellar?'

Vince opened his eyes and sat upright. 'Likely yuh do,' he drawled. 'I sure know you, Glenn.' To McQueen, he added, 'This *hombre* works for the Pinkertons.'

'Got yuh now. Bounty hunter.'

'You objecting?'

'Not me. I'm employed by the railroad, and my brief is to get back the stolen coin.'

Glenn seated himself opposite, watching Jo McQueen and Robbie. 'Never known yuh to work with anyone before, Vince.'

'Lady wants a shot at the Preacher for personal reasons. Robbie's a one-man wagonload of fighting Irish.'

The train rattled and rocked along,

mile after mile, stopping at local stations that seemed no more than a shack in the middle of nowhere, pausing to take on coal or water. Only Robbie enjoyed the journey.

McQueen was feeling disappointed and frustrated, longing to get Preacher in her sights. 'Looks like you guessed wrong, Vince.'

'Or your uncle got it wrong.'

Glenn sat watching them with a bland smile as the train rolled into the depot at the terminus. 'No hold-up,' he said with satisfaction.

'Does that tell yuh something?' Vince asked suspiciously.

The Pinkerton detective nodded. 'There's no coin on this train — the boxes you saw loaded are filled with rocks. That an expected hold-up didn't happen tells me the gang was tipped off. There's a spy at the railroad. Someone on the inside warned them not to bother with this train.'

'Guess you'll be looking for this spy?'

'You got it.'

★ ★ ★

Preacher said, 'Nobody will be expecting a repeat performance just yet. After this, they'll be watching here for a third try — that's when we'll strike elsewhere.'

The train robbers were among the trees near the water tank, waiting for the express car Dan had said would carry more coin.

One man said, doubtfully, 'Hope you're right. With a posse, a bounty man and a Pinkerton all hunting us . . .'

'The Lord is our saviour, have no fear. Dan warned us of the decoy train, didn't he? This is the last place anyone will think to look today. Listen . . .'

Far off, a whistle sounded. Rails hummed. The rattle of an approaching train alerted the Preacher.

'Quiet now. Remain hidden until it stops.'

The train came clanking towards them, slowing, snorting steam and brakes squealing.

It manoeuvred up to the tank and the fireman jumped down from the cab and grabbed the hose. As he inserted the nozzle into the locomotive, Ned rode out from the trees, masked and rifle levelled.

'No tricks,' he warned the engineer. 'Step right down here.'

Preacher advanced confidently with two sticks of dynamite and tied them to the door handle of the express car. He lit a cheroot, sucked till the end glowed and touched it to the fuse. He walked briskly back, pleased; everything was going like clockwork.

There was a double explosion and the door shattered into fragments. Curly moved up with the mules.

One of the guards, dazed, staggered to the doorway holding a rifle. Curly drew fast and shot from the hip, the way he'd been practising. The guard fell backwards, blood soaking the front of his shirt.

'Goddamn you,' the other guard

166

muttered thickly. 'That was cold-blooded murder. I'll see you swing for that!'

Curly only laughed, pleased with his shooting.

Preacher said coldly, 'There was no need for that. Put your gun away and start loading boxes.'

'He could have shot yuh,' the young gunman protested. 'I was only protecting yuh.'

Preacher regarded him with a disgusted expression. 'He was too shaken by the blast to aim straight. Get loading.'

The boxes were strapped to the mules and the cavalcade started towards the river. Preacher went to the front of the train to get Ned.

As they rode off together, Ned said, 'Trouble? I heard a shot.'

Preacher scowled. 'That fool Curly showing off — he had to kill a guard.'

Ned shook his head and sighed. 'You'll need to watch Alder, too — he's one who can't keep away from women.'

Preacher rode in silence, thinking. Curly was a danger to everybody. On the way back, he reviewed various ways he might remove that danger.

* * *

Yale was a careful man, especially when on the trail of wanted desperadoes, but he wasn't feeling too good as he waited high up above the river. Maybe it was something he'd eaten, or he'd caught a chill; whatever, he just didn't feel his usual confident self.

Nothing seemed to be happening so he lay back at ease. The sun was hot, reminding him that rattlesnakes might be out. Maybe the railroad gang would use the river to hide their tracks again — and maybe he was wasting his time.

Sometimes, he thought, Lewis expected miracles. He was one marshal, alone until Lew had shown up at Crow Junction, worried about McQueen.

His eyes closed . . .

Something woke him. Sounds. He rolled into shadow, hoping his horse would remain still and silent. His rifle was in its scabbard on the horse; he had only a single revolver if it came to a fight.

He peered between two rocks. Hoofs clattered on stone as they came up the trail from the river; horses and men, mules loaded with ammunition boxes.

He held his breath, cursing silently. Damn fool! He shouldn't have dropped off to sleep like that. He froze, ignoring an itch that threatened to drive him mad. Still, silent, like a rock.

No alarm sounded, but he heard a voice, 'Keep moving along. The sooner we lose ourselves among the hills the better.'

The cavalcade passed and he breathed easier. He waited till they were out of sight and hearing, collected his horse and followed at a discreet distance. He was feeling better already. He had only to follow and find their hideout, then ride back to collect Lew and a posse. He smiled: easy.

* ★ * ★ * ★

Preacher was turning over ideas in his head; ideas to rid himself of Curly. He rode uphill a little apart from the others, overseeing the mule train, watching and listening. He wasn't sure what alerted him, but something didn't feel right. His suspicions aroused, he took immediate action.

He glanced at the nearest man: O'Brien. 'I'll borrow your rifle,' he said, and held out a hand.

The Irishman looked surprised, but didn't argue.

'Ned, take charge here. I'm dropping back to cover our trail.'

The mules went clattering over the stony path, disappearing behind rocks at a bend. Preacher let them go. There was nothing obvious about his movements but one moment he was visible and the next he was not.

170

He had a vantage point behind a group of rocks that hid him from below, and settled to wait patiently. Minutes passed, then a tiny sound alerted him.

He hadn't been mistaken. He raised his rifle and sighted, waiting for whoever it was to come around the bend.

He saw a man on foot leading a horse. A small man with a mild expression. He didn't look like a man-hunter, but Preacher was not prepared to take a chance. He aimed carefully.

A dead man couldn't talk and he wanted this one to answer a few questions. Besides, he needed a lesson in humility.

He gently squeezed the trigger. The bullet sped true and shattered the small man's knee.

He fell, screaming his agony, rolling about and hugging his leg as tears blinded him.

Preacher moved quickly and, coming up behind him, relieved the small man of his revolver. He used a quirt on the horse to drive it away, downhill. He took the man's water bottle and emptied it on the ground.

Preacher smiled pleasantly and brought out his Bible.

'I can read you the last rites if you wish. Or you might crawl back to the river. Or you might prefer to answer a few questions. Who are you? Who set you to following us?'

The small man stared at him. He began a stream of swear words until Preacher viciously jabbed the muzzle of the rifle against his throat, choking him.

Preacher went through his pockets and found a badge.

'A marshal. I heard one was around the Junction — any more of your kind?'

Yale tried not to moan in front of his tormentor but the pain was too much; he knew he'd never walk without a crutch — if he were allowed to live.

Preacher gestured down the hillside. 'It's a long way to water, marshal . . . and I want to see you crawl.'

Yale muttered something.

'Lewis, is it? Your commissioner, that spawn of Satan.'

Yale went on muttering. 'McQueen'll get yuh — '

'McQueen? Who's McQueen? Answer me!'

Yale spat on his boots and Preacher kicked his shattered knee. He shrieked, and Preacher laughed and brought his horse out of hiding and mounted.

'Better hurry,' he advised the marshal, 'or you'll die of thirst before you get to the river.'

Preacher rode uphill, after the mule train. He experienced a glow of satisfaction as he listened to an enemy of the Lord screaming his way to eternal damnation. The sound was music to his ears.

* * *

News of the latest train robbery burst like a bombshell over Crow Junction. Glenn, cursing, rushed off to the depot

173

to get details. Vince went with him to see if there was anything like a solid trail to follow.

McQueen and Robbie walked to the Drovers' Hotel to find Lew. They sat in the lounge, Lew with whiskey and she and Robbie with a small beer apiece. She was edgy, and that made Robbie nervous.

'Pity Bill went back,' Lew said. 'He'd have enjoyed this.'

'Why? What d'yuh mean?'

'New Pacific's a big organization. Bigheads running it, big money involved. A lot of small people will be laughing fit to bust — robbers ain't always unpopular. Depends who they rob.'

'It's frustrating,' McQueen burst out. 'Preacher's here, within touching distance, and I don't know where. He robs another train and gets clear away. Vince claims the railroad will put up the reward money — and that means more bounty hunters on the trail. And I'm sitting here doing nothing!'

'Resting,' Lew said mildly. 'Building

up your strength while others run around in circles getting nowhere. When you need to move, you'll be fit. Just take it easy for now.'

She flared up. 'I don't want to take it easy — I want Preacher in my sights.'

'I expect yuh do, Jo. But even if you get to him first, he won't be alone. Wait till you get definite word — Yale is out there somewhere, searching.'

Lew looked hard at her. 'Two down and one to go. What then, Jo? Time you started to think forward — what'll you do when Preacher's dead? That's something to think about while you're waiting.'

He finished his whiskey and got up. 'Figure to have a word with Pinkerton's man.'

He left the lounge and McQueen sat there, grim and bitter, staring into a future without meaning.

Robbie watched her anxiously. He didn't know what to say to her, and shifted uneasily in his chair. The chair creaked.

13

A Weak Link

Yale sweated. Partly from the baking heat, partly with fear, but after a while it didn't seem like the Preacher was playing cat and mouse. There was no sound of him coming back to finish him off.

The pain was excruciating every time he tried to move, but he had to get out of direct sunlight before he fried. He clamped his mouth shut, biting down hard; he'd be damned before he let Preacher hear him scream again. He took a long breath and forced himself to roll over into the shade, and passed out.

When he came to, gasping, he groped for his tobacco sack, made a cigarette and struck a match. He lay still, smoking quietly; a small pleasure the Preacher had overlooked. He tried to relax but found it impossible; he was too tense, knowing the slightest movement could start the agony again.

It seemed the Preacher really expected him to die trying to get down to water. Yale would have laughed if his throat wasn't already parched. He might well die, there was no point pretending otherwise, but it would be while crawling uphill after the train robbers. If he could reach the top and mark the route taken by the gang, retribution would follow.

Commissioner Lewis, he knew, wasn't the sort to sit on his hands when one of his men went missing.

He finished his smoke and made up his mind. No matter what the cost in pain, he was going up. Starting now. He tried to save his injured leg by using his hands to drag himself up the stony path. Every inch gained was at the expense of sweat, tears and agony. Blood leaked from his knee and he had to remind himself that the Preacher was getting further away with each second . . .

He passed out; came to and crawled upwards; passed out again.

Once he woke up to find himself facing a rattlesnake. It lay coiled on bare rock, sunbathing, directly in the path before him. They stared at each other, each reluctant to shift, for what seemed hours. He heard no rattle, so it didn't see him as a threat. He waited, staring past his bloody fingertips, admiring the snake's patterning and colouring . . . until it glided silently and smoothly away.

He went on again, ever upwards until, eventually, he found growing things; bushes, a small tree. Yale fished in his shirt pocket. Preacher had made another mistake in overlooking his pocket-knife. He unfolded the blade and selected a stout branch he could just reach. He sawed at it, gritting his teeth as he hauled himself up on one leg.

The branch began to give way as he leaned on it, and he fell, sobbing; but he had a stick that would take his weight. He rested, then removed his shirt and folded it again and again to make a pad to go in the pit of his arm. Now he had a crutch.

He limped along until he passed out. When he regained consciousness, the sky was darkening and he could no longer see a trail to follow.

* * *

'Not this time,' Preacher said. 'I'm taking Curly with me.'

Ned was surprised and gave him a sharp look. 'Dan won't like that. He knows me.'

The train robbers were taking their ease in that part of the abandoned fort that had standing walls and most of a roof. One of them had made a kitchen area stocked with groceries; bedrolls were laid out against the walls.

'With a Pinkerton in town, Dan may already be under suspicion,' Preacher pointed out.

179

'Me?' Even Curly seemed surprised.

'You fancy yourself as a gunman, don't you? We may have to shoot our way out.'

Curly strutted, proud of his moment of glory as Ned handed him a canvas bag filled with gold coins; Dan's share of the loot.

'You're in charge, Ned.'

Preacher and Curly brought their horses from ruined stabling, open to the sky, and started downhill. The fort was fifty feet up on a rocky crag, the land below exposed on all sides. No one could creep up on them unobserved.

Preacher picked up a faint trail and they jogged along easily, swinging a wide loop to make it harder for anyone to backtrack them.

Preacher remained silent, pondering over the marshal's last words. McQueen? Who the hell was McQueen? The name meant nothing to him.

It was dark when they approached Crow Junction, and Preacher slowed his horse to a walk and reined in behind the depot, among shadowed buildings. The noise from Main Street's saloons was faint and distant.

Preacher stayed in the saddle as Curly dismounted and hitched his horse. 'Be still,' he hissed. 'I thought I heard something.'

Curly paused, hand resting on the butt of his holstered revolver, peering into the gloom. 'Reckon you're a mite nervous,' he said scornfully. 'I'll go in on my own if you're scared.'

Preacher spoke in hardly more than a whisper. 'Stay away from Dan's door until I'm sure the way's clear. I don't want him nailed along with you.'

Curly snorted and walked forward, revolver in one hand and the bag of coins in the other.

Preacher quietly dismounted and stood behind his horse in the shadows. He had his Bible in his hands and waited patiently. As a shout came from the shadows: 'Hands up!' He opened the Bible.

Curly swung around, firing in the

direction of the voice. Lead blasted back. A door opened and yellow light shone out, silhouetting him.

Preacher shot once and Curly went down, hit in the back. He walked his horse quietly away, attracting no attention as other doors opened and voices shouted an alarm.

A few more shots, fired at random, hit nobody. Whoever was shooting couldn't see well enough to find a target. Presently, a voice with some authority in it, bawled, 'Stop shooting, you damned fools!'

An excited crowd gathered, drawn by the sound of gunshots. Curly lay face down, unmoving, canvas bag open and a shower of gold coins spilled on the ground.

'It's one of the train robbers!'

Preacher continued to move slowly and quietly away. He swung into his saddle with a prayer on his lips: 'Lord, help thy servant in his hour of need.'

No one caught on there was a second man; the excitement behind him gradually died away.

Once clear of the Junction he put his horse to the gallop and merged with the night, satisfied that Curly was no longer a danger to anyone.

* * *

Vince led them slowly, circling out from the depot in an early morning light, looking for tracks. McQueen followed on Nemesis, who felt frisky and wanted to run; she had continually to hold him back. Robbie, on his mule, plodded along after her.

The bounty hunter grunted his satisfaction. 'As I thought, a second man. I was suspicious as soon as I inspected the body and saw he'd been shot in the back.'

'Thieves fall-out?' McQueen suggested.

'Something like that. Who cares?'

Further on, Vince said, 'He's trying to hide his tracks. It'll be slow work from now on, but there's no doubt he's headed for the hills. Let's get up high.'

They set their animals to climbing between the trees to the crest and rode along the ridge of the range. From time to time Vince paused to look through his telescope.

'Draw an imaginary line from the railroad water tank,' he said. 'Draw another imaginary line from the depot. I reckon, where those two lines cross is the right area to search.'

The sun warmed up and they paused at a spring to let their mounts drink, and refill their water bottles.

Vince said, 'Wherever they're holed up, they can't be far from water. We'll move over towards the river — it would be useful to find where they came up from the valley.'

They ate dry rations and moved on, keeping to the high places and looking down. Suddenly Vince reined back and stared through his telescope. He looked hard and then handed the glass to McQueen.

'See what you think.'

She focused. 'Looks like a body.'

'But whose? And why there?'

They rode down the slope and approached warily. 'If he's not a goner,' Vince drawled, 'he's next door to it.'

Robbie's face had an anxious look as he rode closer and got down from his mule. He felt shock when he saw the state of the knee, mangled beyond anything a doctor could hope to save. Then he realized the man was breathing.

He unslung his leather water bottle and crouched, holding the man's head and shoulders upright. He fed a trickle of liquid into the corner of a gaping mouth. McQueen joined him.

'Needs help,' Robbie said.

McQueen remained silent. Vince stayed on his horse, watching the land all around. There was no sign of a wandering horse or dropped gun.

The injured man opened his eyes and croaked, 'Water.'

Robbie gave him another small amount. 'No more just yet,' he said firmly.

The unknown man closed his eyes, swallowed, and opened them again.

'Followed train robbers up . . . Preacher ambushed me.'

'That sounds like Preacher,' McQueen said.

He fumbled in a pocket and brought out a deputy US marshal's badge. 'Yale. Let Commissioner Lewis know. Crow Junction.'

She stared. 'You're Yale, and I owe you. I'm McQueen.'

Vince was casting around for tracks. 'At least now we have a starting point.'

Robbie cut two straight sticks from a tree for splints, and warned, 'This is going to hurt.'

Vince volunteered a slug of whiskey from his flask, then Robbie bound up the injured limb. His big hands were amazingly gentle, but even so the patient passed out. He lifted Yale easily on to his mule and tied him in place.

McQueen realized that Robbie showed a sure knowledge of what was needed and went ahead as if he were in charge.

'You stay with Vince, Jo,' he said. 'I'll

take Mr Yale into town to the doc and report to Mr Lewis. Then I'll come back and find you again.'

He walked away, taking giant strides, leading his mule with Yale slumped in the saddle.

* * *

Lew sat with Glenn on a bench outside the Drovers' Hotel. They were in the shade and each had a drink handy. The Pinkerton man was trying to persuade him to put pressure on Daniels.

'I've got a feeling about Mr Daniels. He carries a grudge against the railroad — and he's one of the few who knew which train carried the gold.'

'Promising,' Lew said mildly. 'But you lack proof. Set a watch on him.'

'I reckon we'd soon get an admission if we leaned on him, just a little.'

Lew smiled pleasantly. 'The law isn't too keen on that and, in case you've forgotten, I represent the law.'

Glenn's bulldog jaw pushed forward.

'That's why I'm glad I work for a private firm. We're not tied down by rules and regulations. We can — '

He broke off, staring along the dusty street. 'Is that big Robbie? Walking?'

Lew glimpsed the body of a rider slumped in the saddle of the mule Robbie was leading. He grabbed his cane and limped into the road as fast as he could.

He saw it wasn't Jo, and relaxed; then recognised Yale and yelled to Glenn: 'Get the doc here, pronto.'

He took a long look at the marshal's knee and swore bitterly. 'What happened to him, for God's sake?'

'Preacher shot him.'

The town doctor, when he arrived, made up his mind quickly. 'There's no way I can repair that kind of damage. He needs hospital treatment.'

Lew said, 'When's the next train leaving?'

Glenn consulted his watch. 'Luckily, in under an hour.'

'Get him along to the depot, Robbie.'

'Yes, sir. Than I'll head straight back to Jo.'

'Do that.'

As Lew helped them load Yale aboard the train, Glenn asked, 'Does that change your mind?'

Lew wasn't smiling now. He gave a curt nod. 'Let's interview Daniels.'

★ ★ ★

McQueen followed Vince at a discreet distance as he tried to read sign. The bounty hunter moved slowly, watching the ground with hawk eyes as he tried to find the way the railroad robbers had taken.

She was uneasy, her expression bleak, as she realized she was reluctant to be alone with Vince. She'd not felt that way about Robbie, and was unhappy she'd allowed herself to trust the big man. The bounty man was very different; she got the impression he didn't care for anyone except himself.

Vince sat back and rubbed his eyes.

'It's no good. I've lost it. We'll have to go up again and spy out the land.'

They rode up to the crest and followed the ridge till he stopped to use his telescope. He handed her the glass.

'Recognize him?'

She had a job focusing at first but then, suddenly, a man on horseback far below loomed large in the glass and almost near enough to touch. A man dressed in black with his hat pushed back far enough to reveal flame-coloured hair.

'*Preacher!*'

She knew the face from her nightmare, remembered it looming above her, a gaunt face with no hint of mercy. She remembered her father. She felt loathing and fury and hatred building up inside her and raised her rifle to firing position.

Vince caught her hand just in time. 'No! The range is too great. You'd only warn him.'

Reluctantly she lowered her rifle. She sat watching until the rider disappeared among trees on a hillside. Vince cast about to pick up his trail but they didn't see him again.

Presently, the bounty hunter asked, 'How bad d'yuh want him? Bad enough to act as bait?'

McQueen didn't hesitate. 'Yes. Anything.'

'We're close, I'm sure of that. A woman might tempt one of them to make a grab. And then,' he closed his hand to make a fist, 'I can make him lead us straight to them.'

* * *

Glenn said, 'Not many people knew which train the coin was travelling on. You're one of them.'

Daniels smiled derisively. 'You wish. A lot more people knew than you imagine. It's hard to keep a secret where money's involved.'

They were crowded into a back room at the depot, and it was warm with the door shut. There were the remains of a meal on the table. The view from a tiny

191

window showed only the blank wall of a shed.

The Pinkerton man was asking the questions, with Lew listening in. He wondered how tough Glenn was; so far the gloves were on.

Remembering Yale, Lew was getting impatient. He'd been one of the roughest marshals on the frontier, and Jo wanted the Preacher. He noticed how Daniels favoured his bad arm.

He picked up a metal knife lying across a plate. He reversed it to grip it by the blade, leaned across the table and slammed the heavy handle down on that arm.

Daniels screamed.

'Sorry,' Lew said blandly. 'Guess my hand sort of slipped. Be too bad now if I broke the other arm. With two useless arms I sure reckon the railroad wouldn't have much need of yuh.'

Daniels began to sweat, and Glenn smiled. 'I'll leave him with yuh for a while, Lew. That way, there'll be no witness if he has an accident.' He started for the door.

'No, don't leave me with him. I — '

Glenn paused. 'You know, if I hinted to New Pacific that I suspected you of being the spy, they'd double-quick sack yuh. You were going to say?'

Daniels mumbled something under his breath, and Glenn continued, 'No pension and no job. You might have to start spending those gold coins. Someone would talk and I'd be waiting to pounce.'

Daniels' face was pale, and he looked from one man to the other and saw no mercy in either. He stared at the floor.

'It's not right — I should have got a pension. I worked for this railroad for years. My arm was busted on the job and — '

'Stop whining,' Lew said, 'or I'll give yuh something to whine about!'

Glenn moved close and stood over him with a menacing attitude as he nursed his bad arm.

'Your bunch of train robbers shot a guard and he died. That's murder — and you're tied in with them — so it's a hanging job. I might, just might, be able to help yuh if you tell me where their hideout is.'

'The Preacher's a murderer several times over,' Lew added. 'I want him real bad and I don't give a damn what happens to you. You can save yourself a lot of unpleasantness by talking.'

Daniels was beginning to look desperate. Glenn said, 'If I get the money back, I'll maybe forget you were involved.'

Lew leaned forward. 'Yeah, tell us where their hideout is and we'll let yuh go. Any life is better than none.'

Daniels' face ran with sweat. 'Preacher would kill me — '

Lew turned away in disgust. 'All right, forget it. I'll tour the saloons, get a few gents liquored up and bring 'em back here with a rope.' He started towards the door. 'No need for the cost of a trial.'

'No . . . no . . . ' Daniels finally broke down. 'It's an old army fort up in the hills.'

14

Live Bait

Jo McQueen hesitated. It was one thing to go after the Preacher and shoot from cover. It was quite another to act as bait, to ride out alone and wait for him to come to her.

Then she remembered young Pike, and smiled: let him come. If he, or any other man — even Vince — got near enough, she'd use her knife on him.

She rode slowly down the hillside, in the open; a lamb to tempt the wolves. There was a faint track and she kept to that, knowing Robbie was back and moving after her under cover of the trees. He'd worried about her, but had finally seen the sense behind Vince's argument; they had to lure someone out to answer questions.

The bounty man remained on a

hilltop with his telescope. She was acutely aware that neither of them could reach her in time if she came under serious attack but, hopefully, one man might be tempted to show himself by a woman on her own. Assuming the train robbers bothered to keep a watch. And if she could get close to him . . .

It was hot in the open and she tipped her hat forward to shade her eyes. The air was still and quiet.

A rider appeared from the trees, cutting across her path.

McQueen's heart beat faster and she reined in the stallion.

'Hi! On your own? What yuh doing here?' His voice held suspicion and his gaze roamed around the valley before settling on her. 'Yeah, I thought so. A woman, and all alone . . .'

'You don't have to be afraid,' she said calmly. 'Surely you're not scared of women? I might ask you the same question: what are you doing here? It's pretty isolated.'

He was leering now. 'Sure is.' He

edged his horse nearer. Obviously he liked what he saw. He was not the Preacher, but it was a safe assumption he was one of the gang. That meant the hideout must be close by.

He was short, broad across the chest, and smiling like a cat that'd found a bowl of cream. He gave another quick look around to make sure nobody else was in sight.

'Reckon you don't have to hurry away now we've met. My name's Alder, and it sure does seem the ladies like me well enough to dawdle awhile. Why don't we just find a secluded spot among the trees and — '

All the time he was speaking his horse had been drifting closer till he could lunge across and make a grab at her.

'Got — '

McQueen tensed, smelling the whiskey on his breath. She knew a moment of panic, her nightmare returning, then her knife was out of its sheath and slashing wildly at the hand gripping her.

Alder howled and his horse started back. He stared at the blood dripping from his wrist, and cursed, 'You cut me, you damned bitch!'

He came out of his saddle and ran at her, grabbing her leg to pull her down. She slashed again, but still he threw her to the ground.

Nemesis bared his teeth, then backed off as a mule came charging out from the trees, crashing through undergrowth like an express train.

Robbie hit the ground running and couldn't stop. He had a lot of momentum. His weight and speed hit Alder with the force of an enraged buffalo, hurling him across the ground. Robbie landing on top of him was a shock like that of a falling tree. His hands went around Alder's neck and shook him as though he were nothing more than a rag doll.

Alder didn't protest because he couldn't.

McQueen was taking deep breaths to calm herself when Vince arrived.

The bounty hunter looked at the train robber and shook his head sadly. 'You surely don't know your strength, Robbie. You can get up and leave him now.'

McQueen said, 'Robbie didn't mean to kill him.'

Vince shrugged. 'Wa'al, that one sure ain't goin' to open his mouth. I wonder when they'll send his relief?'

* * *

After touring a selection of Crow Junction's saloons, Lew and Glenn had failed to find a guide to direct them to the abandoned fort. It had, apparently, been long forgotten. They got blank stares and the offer of a drink, but no information.

'I could likely borrow a map from the nearest army post,' Lew said, 'but that would mean more delay.'

In the next saloon, a greying barkeep suggested: 'Look for 'Happy' Harrison — he used to be an army sergeant, till he retired.'

'And where will we find him?'

'He spends his time drinking his pension, mostly in the Last Dollar. He would know, if anyone does, if you can sober him up.'

Lew and Glenn continued along Main Street to the end, where the no-hopers existed. They saw sod huts and tents. The Last Dollar was the final saloon before the Junction petered out at the edge of the prairie.

It looked dingy and ramshackle; inside there were no girls and no music. Some Boot Hills Lew had known were livelier.

There was one bar, with liquor behind it, for solitary drinkers, when they had any money. There were six tables between the bar and the door, but only two were occupied. A few men sat slumped before empty glasses. Nobody spoke, but a few looked hopefully towards Lew and Glenn as they entered. There was not even a card school in progress.

The man behind the bar stopped

yawning; he appeared surprised to see a new face.

'Looking for Harrison — '

A body lifted its head from a table. 'Sergeant, seven-three-one,' a slurred voice said. 'Reporting for duty, sir.'

The face was composed of broken veins with a large red nose that had run into a door. The clothes were rumpled and smelly.

Lew said, 'We want to get to the abandoned fort in the hills. Can you guide us there?'

'Why not? Served years there, didn't I?'

'But can you find it now?'

'Find it in my sleep,' Harrison mumbled.

'I'm a United States marshal and will pay you the going rate, afterwards. This fellar with me is one of Pinkerton's men. We're chasing the railroad robbers and believe they've made the old fort their headquarters.'

'Some nerve!' Harrison said, indignantly. He lurched upright, attempting a salute. 'Rely on me, sir. I'll guide yuh.'

'The gang's leader is an army deserter — '

'Is he now?' Harrison made an obvious attempt to get a grip on himself. 'We show no mercy to deserters — just lead me to him.'

Glenn said drily, 'We were hoping you could lead us to him.'

'Lead yuh straight there.'

Lew doubted the way would be straight, but nobody else claimed to know. Harrison swayed towards the door, helped by Lew and Glenn, one on each side.

'I'll just get my horse and water bottle — '

'This way, sergeant.'

Lew guided him towards the horse trough and ducked his head under again and again.

Harrison spluttered for air, shaking water off the way a dog does. 'What d'yuh do that for?'

'Thought you might appreciate a

clear head to remember the route is all, Sergeant.'

'Find it blindfold in my sleep,' Harrison said, with every appearance of confidence.

They walked up Main Street. A posse was gathering, composed of townsmen, the sheriff and his deputies and another bounty hunter.

They milled around in the middle of the street, armed to the teeth. The local doctor joined them.

Lew shouted for quiet. 'Listen! I'm the law and I'm in charge. Anyone objecting to that can drop out now. We're going up against murderers so I don't want you treating this as a junket. I want each one of you back with a whole skin.'

Lew pushed Harrison up front and the sergeant croaked, 'Company, advance.' He led out from Crow Junction towards the hills, murdering 'The Girl I Left Behind Me.'

Lew looked at Glenn, and grimaced. 'It's the one out in front I worry about.'

★　★　★

After Alder attacked her, McQueen withdrew into herself. She feared sleep, knowing the nightmare would return. They moved deep among the trees and made a cold camp; Vince wouldn't allow a fire.

It was biscuits and water and a blanket under a leafy canopy, starlight and a rustle of leaves as the wind shifted.

She glimpsed Robbie's large bulk curled up with the animals and the bounty hunter had no problem sleeping. He'd insisted on letting Alder's horse go, leaving the body where it lay: an unexplained mystery to worry the Preacher's men.

But eventually her eyes closed and it started again. Preacher riding up to the homestead, this time with Alder. Again the Bible changed into a gun that spat death. Again her mother was pistol-whipped before she was killed.

Again she writhed each time a stubbled

face leered above her, breathing whiskey fumes. Again came Preacher's mocking voice echoing like the tattoo on a drum, 'Woman, you will obey, obey, obey . . . '

There was pain, and blood and she screamed her hatred to the night clouds.

Robbie woke, troubled, and rose to go to her, but Vince laid a hand on his shoulder.

'Not right this moment, Robbie. You need to let her live through this by herself because she won't know yuh at all. She sleeps with one hand on that knife — you wake her suddenly and she'll gut yuh like she would a turkey.'

He paused, reflecting, 'You know, I feel almost sorry for that Preacher fellar.'

15

The Abandoned Fort

The Preacher forced himself to remain calm; after all, he was the one with brains. He was considering their next hold-up, but no one else seemed interested, or even listening. They had other things on their mind; like Curly's death, and now Alder's.

And, of course, they had money to spend and wanted to hit town and celebrate.

Alder's death was still a mystery. His horse had been found unharmed and grazing quietly not far from the mangled body. They had found the tracks of a mule — but it was ridiculous to imagine a mule had savaged him.

Preacher found himself wondering about the unknown 'McQueen' the marshal had mentioned. He frowned as someone said, 'Why don't we split up and go different ways?'

They were sitting close around a small fire that didn't show outside the fort, passing a bottle from hand to hand. Evening shadows thickened. The air was still. Preacher let them talk. Talk meant nothing.

Someone else asked, 'You reckon Dan will still give us a tip-off? After Curly?'

'Of course he will,' Preacher said quickly. 'I'm not sure who got Curly, because the shot came from the shadows, but Dan wasn't involved at all.'

He looked towards Ned for support. 'Once we get the tip-off, I want to stop the train somewhere else — another part of the track. They won't be expecting that.'

'Is there any point in coming back here?' Ned asked.

'This fort is too good to leave,' Preacher said firmly. 'It commands the high ground. Nobody can get at us without being seen — and we can hold out if anyone should come this way. It's a natural.'

'The way Alder was killed wasn't natural.'

'Sure wasn't. I'm not patrolling alone — you can forget that.'

Preacher said, irritated, 'It was just some wild animal got him.'

The mystery of Alder's death had upset them. No one was going to admit to being scared, but no one left the circle of light thrown by the fire. No one wanted to curl up in a blanket by the outer wall in the dark.

Evening merged into night; the hours passed and the air grew colder. Men dozed around a dying fire. Outside the woods were full of shadows. Even the Preacher had to shut from his mind old campfire tales of Indian graveyards and the night stalker they called the Wendigo.

Then came a scream, the like of which no man had heard before. It came from the trees and froze muscles

208

and tightened nerves and turned blood to ice.

They spooked, scrambling upright and grabbing weapons. They formed a ring about the fire, facing outwards, wild-eyed and staring desperately into shadowed areas. It was after midnight and the air felt suddenly chill. Scalps tightened and sweat was cold.

The scream went on and on, a long drawn out wailing cry of mounting intensity bringing the promise of terror with it. It was an awful screech, desolate, filling them with dismay.

Preacher watched them with contempt; he was not unmoved by the weird howling, but refused to give way to fear. In the moonlight, they froze into a death-like stillness.

'What on earth's that?' someone mumbled.

'A banshee,' O'Brien said solemnly. 'Aye, 'tis a haunt from the Old Country, no doubt about it. A premonition and a warning. It means another death.'

They stared down into the dark woods and trembled.

'Saint Patrick save us,' murmured the Irishman.

When the scream finally faded to leave a silence both cold and fearful, Preacher poured scorn on the idea.

'You pack of superstitious fools! That was only the cry of some wild animal.'

'Was it now? And can you put a name to any animal that screams like that?'

Preacher had no ready answer. 'If it bothers you, we'll set a guard.

'Up here,' he added quickly. 'While you follow me, you have nothing to fear — the Lord is my shield, as he is yours.'

No one laughed, but he had to put out his best performance to quieten nerves before they settled again; though he never quite managed to silence his own doubts. He put more wood on the fire to build it up and sat, shivering, with a blanket wrapped about his shoulders.

* * *

It takes an army man to know one, Harrison thought, and there's not another in this outfit. The idea made him happy and he took an extra sip from his canteen. Anyone who'd been in the army would have guessed it wasn't water he was tasting.

But he took only a small sip and recorked the bottle. It had to last out the trip and he didn't want that damned marshal to suspect anything. That one took life altogether too seriously. A little drink never hurt anybody. And always trying to hurry the posse along, even though he didn't know the way. What did it matter if a bunch of thieves milked the railroad? Good luck to 'em!

One thing was sure: 'Happy' Harrison wouldn't be in the forefront if they caught up with this gang. What mattered was the feeling of importance guiding the posse gave him, because he was the only one who knew the lie of the land and exactly where the old fort was.

Knowing he was needed again gave him a warm feeling. In the old days, a sergeant was an important man — he hadn't enjoyed being dumped like garbage at the end of his service; nor being regarded as the town drunk. He'd resented it, and now was regaining his self-respect.

There was no hurry, as far as he was concerned; the longer he took to find the fort the longer he was somebody again.

The path he took between the trees wound steadily upwards. He couldn't make his delaying tactics too obvious or someone might catch on.

He paused again to look around. 'Looking for the next landmark,' he explained. 'Should be about here somewhere. It's been a while since I was this way.'

'The land doesn't change that much.' Lew snapped.

'Wa'al, it seems to change — my memory ain't what it used to be.'

Lew put a curb on his impatience.

'Try to hurry along, will yuh?'

'Sure thing,' Harrison agreed, and took another sip.

The trail continued to meander among the hills. The sun burned. One by one some of the townsmen lost their enthusiasm and dropped out. The posse shrank. The doctor, with his carpetbag of tools and remedies, moved up to join Lew and Glenn and the bounty hunter.

The sun turned red as it dropped below the line of hills. Shadows grew among the trees when Harrison reined back near a small creek, where bushes reached almost to its bank.

'Company, halt!'

Swaying in the saddle, he grinned at Lew. 'We'll camp here tonight. Tomorrow, I figure we'll sight the fort.'

Lew watched suspiciously as the sergeant dismounted unsteadily. He passed close to Harrison and, as their guide breathed out, he breathed in. The smell of whiskey was so strong he almost gagged. The man was drunk.

Lew felt disgusted with himself; he

should have suspected earlier. Jo was out there somewhere, looking for Preacher, and he should be with her.

He muttered to Glenn, 'Help Sergeant Harrison collect firewood. We need coffee and a hot meal.'

The Pinkerton man was startled for a moment, till Lew closed one eye. Then he urged the sergeant towards the trees.

Once his back was turned, Lew grabbed the sergeant's water bottle from his saddle and emptied it on the ground. He walked to the creek, knelt and refilled it.

They sat around the fire as darkness came, eating and spreading their blankets. Lew watched Harrison reach for his water bottle, and thought: 'Maybe tomorrow he'll take a straight line to the fort.'

★ ★ ★

Vince made a smokeless fire, just big enough to cook bacon and beans and boil coffee. Robbie sat beside him, waiting patiently, peering towards the creek where McQueen was washing off the night's sweat. He looked anxious.

Vince glanced up as she approached. Short dark hair still wet and plastered down, skin a nut-brown, she might almost pass for an Indian. Her trail clothes were worn and dusty; dressed up, he supposed, she might be halfway attractive.

She said, 'I'm fine now, Robbie, so you can stop worrying. It was a nightmare — I've had them before.'

Yeah, Vince thought, but not for much longer if I'm guessing right. A hard woman. He wondered where she'd met Preacher, and why she reacted so violently, but he sure as hell wasn't going to ask.

He dished up breakfast and they ate in silence.

As a bounty hunter, he'd come up against some rough *hombres*; men he'd had to disarm before he approached. A few, those wanted dead or alive and desperate, he'd shot from cover; and all the time he'd had to get ahead of other bounty men as tough as himself.

But McQueen was one he intended never to tangle with. It occurred to him that he hadn't once seen her smile. And right now she appeared as lean and hungry as the leader of a wolf pack going for the throat.

Vince had been a loner all his life, one of those who had difficulty fitting in anywhere. And he had learnt to cope. But now he had this strange pair in tow and didn't understand them at all. He wondered what he'd got himself into and whether it had all been a mistake.

One thing he was sure of; she was dangerous to be around and he was growing increasingly wary. He had best not be between her and the Preacher when the showdown came; after all, he only wanted the reward money.

He wondered about Robbie too; the size of him was enough to make any man uneasy. Sure, he was a dummy, but the way he got along with that big stallion was an eye-opener. Vince took care to avoid the mean-looking brute.

When they set off again, they moved in single file, with McQueen on Nemesis in the middle and Vince leading. From time to time he stopped to spy through his glass; other times there was a faint trail to follow.

He was careful to move under cover of the trees; he had the exciting feeling they were very close now.

'No singing, Robbie,' he warned. 'Make as little noise as possible.'

They were coming to an open area and he paused in shade to study the next hill. There were ruins at the top of what might be an old army fort.

He used his telescope. 'Interesting. What do you think?'

He passed the instrument to McQueen and she took her time studying what was left of the building. 'Someone there,' she said, passing the glass to Robbie. 'I think we can be pretty sure who it is.'

All three studied the open hillside.

'How do we get up there?'

'We don't,' Vince said. 'Not alive. Keep under the trees — we'll circle around.'

They moved slowly and carefully but eventually got all the way around the hill; every side was bare.

Vince reined back under the trees by a small creek. He smiled and stroked his beard.

'This'll do us. They're going to need water, so we'll wait for someone to come down. And pick them off, one by one.'

16

The Downhill Fight

Sergeant Harrison kept the posse moving fast and straight next morning. So fast some had a problem keeping up. Lew smirked; he'd only had to promise the sergeant all the whiskey he could drink once they reached the fort.

After getting over his sulk, Harrison realized this was his best chance for getting his next drink, and urged his horse to speed. As he neared their target, his tongue was almost hanging out and his body craved hard liquor.

'There!' he shouted, pointing forward. 'See it? Up top!'

Lew gazed up, studying the ruin on the crest of a hill just ahead. Glenn looked thoughtful. 'Too open for a charge,' he said.

Harrison licked his lips. 'So where's the whiskey?'

Lew nodded towards the fort. 'Up there, I've no doubt. You ever hear of a crooked outfit that didn't have a cache of whiskey? Help yourself.'

The sergeant looked stunned. 'But — '

'Shouldn't take long to rout that gang, with you leading us.'

Lew rode on, and then McQueen walked out from under the trees. 'Uncle Lew! Preacher's here, I'm almost sure. We saw him riding this way, but lost him.'

He felt a surge of relief. She hadn't lost all sense and moved against the gang alone.

'Right. Let's get under cover. They have all the advantage at the moment.'

'Not quite all,' Vince drawled, showing himself, and indicating a small creek. 'Depends how much water they have.'

'Water!' Harrison gave a bitter laugh.

'They don't need water if they've got whiskey!'

The bounty man who'd ridden with the posse was scowling. 'You here too, Vince?'

'Where else should I be? And ahead of you, Smitty.'

Robbie moved up alongside Vince.

Lew said, mildly, 'Now, boys, take it easy. We're all together in this. You're each part of a legal posse under federal law and we're up against a bunch of killers. We can't afford to quarrel amongst ourselves.'

He waited a moment while men and horses settled. 'Everyone under cover? Good.'

He stepped into the open alone, and fired a shot to grab attention. He made a funnel with his hands, and shouted:

'You, in the fort. I represent federal law, and I'm here with a deputized posse. If you surrender now, you'll get a fair trial before a judge.'

There was a short pause, then a barrage of gunfire came from above.

221

Lew limped among the trees and sheltered behind a solid trunk.

A voice echoed, mocking: 'Come and get us, lawman!'

Another hail of bullets shredded the leaves.

Lew glanced at Glenn, and nodded. 'Reckon Vince called it right. We hold the creek, and wait.'

* * *

Preacher felt almost sick with disgust. All his planning, his time spent nursing these idiots along, gone for nothing.

'Fools,' he raged. 'I'm surrounded by fools. I told you — '

'That was Alder,' Ned said quietly. 'You gave that job to Alder. Guess we all forgot when we discovered what happened to him.'

O'Brien chimed in, 'Except we still don't know exactly what did happen.'

Preacher ground his teeth. 'The fact remains, we're short of water and there's a posse camped by the creek. If our barrels were full — and I gave orders they should be — we could sit here and wait them out. They can't get at us. They'd get tired of waiting and go away.'

'Maybe,' someone muttered.

Preacher glared at a circle of stubbled faces.

Each face looked serious, but not one man offered to go down to carry a bucket of water up. The hillside was too exposed. What had seemed an advantage proved, with a posse's guns covering the creek, to be a trap.

They were safe behind the walls of the fort, but they couldn't last long without a water supply.

Ned said, 'I've been watching. I don't reckon there's so many of them; maybe fewer than we are. I reckon, if we ride down shooting as we go, we could break through and get clear away. I say rush them.'

'That might be possible,' Preacher agreed, 'but you're forgetting the weight of gold. D'yuh want to leave that behind?'

'Not likely!'

'But now they know we're here, more men are likely to arrive and join them.'

Ned looked unhappy. 'We've got the gold — but we're likely to lose it, and our lives.'

O'Brien said, 'Wa'al, I'm going. A few coins in my pocket and ride like hell. Live to rob another train is my idea.'

'You're crazy! I'm not leaving gold behind!'

'They're sure to catch you if yuh carry too heavy a load.'

Preacher toured the walls, gazing down, and came to a decision.

'All right,' he said abruptly. 'We'll go together in a bunch as soon as the light fades — we know these trails and they don't. We can lose them in the dark.'

* * *

McQueen studied the sky and said, 'It'll be dark in an hour. Suppose they make a break for it? They don't have to come down this side.'

Vince smiled. 'Maybe not, but I'm staying right here beside this creek.'

Lew thought about it. 'Maybe. I think Vince has the right idea — but, still, in the dark they might try to swing around and come at us from behind. It's obvious where we are, so some of you spread out a bit.'

'You know,' the Pinkerton detective murmured. 'In the dark we could sneak up there. That gold coin is my end of the job.'

'Me, too,' a dry throat croaked.

They waited, resting easy till the sun began to hide behind the hills. McQueen took the stallion's reins and led Nemesis between the trees, circling around towards the back side of the hill. Robbie followed her like a shadow.

She paused beneath a leafy tree, staring up the slope. The land appeared different as the light went. If the gang came now, she thought, it was going to be difficult to aim accurately.

She strained to make out the silhouette of the fort, and listened intently. Was that a jingle of harness?

* ★ ★ *

Preacher ate sparingly and moistened his lips with water. Some of the gang were eating as though it might be their last meal; others were at the whiskey.

'Only one drink,' Preacher advised. 'And only a few coins in your pocket. Obviously, most of the posse will stay close to the creek, so we'll ride down the far side of the hill.'

'We could bury the rest of the gold,' one hopeful suggested. 'And come back for it later.'

'You really believe a posseman won't think of that?'

Shadows lengthened. Quietly they brought their horses from the ruined stabling, checked their guns and mounted. They waited, their pockets heavy with gold coins.

Preacher sat relaxed, watching the

sunlight fade, thinking of the marshal's words, 'McQueen'll get yuh.' Maybe McQueen was down there, somewhere in the darkness. Maybe he was another marshal. Did it matter now?

He kneed his horse forward, to the brink of the slope, holding aloft his Bible. 'All right — *ride!*'

They started down the hillside, gathering speed. Preacher shouted, 'Hallelujah, and confusion to the enemies of the Lord!'

A single gunshot boomed out.

★ ★ ★

Lew asked suddenly, 'What's that?'

A voice murmured, 'Sure sounds like horses.'

Lew stared into a glimmer of rapidly fading light that showed between the trunks of trees beside the creek. For a moment, a sound had overlaid that of trickling water. Then he heard a rifle shot. Just one; obviously a warning.

Damn, the gang must be coming

down the far side, where Jo was. He made out a thunder of hoofs, horses working up to a full gallop, and a barrage of gunshots.

Lew nearly had a heart attack. Cursing, he grabbed for the reins of his horse and swung into the saddle. He spurred the animal to speed, yelling back: 'Doc, follow me!'

He was sure now he'd made an error of judgement; Preacher and his gang were intent on busting out and only Jo stood between them and freedom. He pushed his horse hard, a risky thing on unknown ground in the dark where a gopher-hole could break a leg. He crashed through undergrowth, sweating blood.

He told himself he was a stupid old fool, waiting in the wrong place and putting her life at risk. It was too late now; if anything had happened to her it already had and he'd never forgive himself.

He whipped his horse to a cruel pace; he'd never felt so desperate, so hopeless.

Leaves thrashed his face. Small branches were spikes that snapped off as he charged past.

Must be getting past it, he thought. If he couldn't do better than this it was time to retire. And, by God, he would.

★ ★ ★

McQueen heard the pounding of hoofs as they came downhill, faster and faster, working up to a gallop. She fired a warning shot, and bullets came flying back. Horsemen seemed to be pouring down the slope like a tidal wave, firing as they came.

And, somewhere in that mass of moving shadows was the Preacher. She heard his voice ring out, 'Hallelujah, and confusion to the enemies of the Lord!'

She caught a glimpse of a long black coat with the tails flying, hatless and waving a Bible in the air as he passed, going full tilt.

Hatred flared like a volcano about to

explode. *Now!* She snapped off a shot and then kept firing until her rifle was empty. Robbie, a bulky shadow beside her, triggered his revolver. Lead flew back like buzzing hornets.

Then the horsemen swept past and disappeared into the darkness. She thought one went down, but couldn't be sure.

'Robbie, I'm going after — '

There was no answer, but Nemesis made a solid shape in the shadows.

McQueen looked around. Robbie was down, a huge bulk on the ground. Panic hit her. Robbie — hit?

Of course, he was a big target, difficult to miss even in poor light. She cursed viciously. Preacher was getting away and there was no one else near enough to help. She needed to get after the Preacher but she couldn't leave Robbie. She felt sick as an emotional see-saw rocked her first one way, then the other. Leave, stay . . . leave, stay . . . leave, stay . . .

It was a moment that stunned her.

Her whole life seemed to change. She hadn't realized the big man had come to mean so much to her. Thoughts of the Preacher faded beside the need to help Robbie.

She dropped to her knees beside him.

17

Nemesis

Flame stabbed the night air and lead whined about his ears as Preacher spurred his mount to a gallop. He crouched low, hugging his horse's mane. Bullets passed close, but he manoeuvred to keep one of the gang between himself and the marksmen. He was sure he was going to make it when a random slug brought his horse to its knees, and he somersaulted over its head and hit the ground.

The breath was knocked out of him by the impact. His head rang like a bell and he lay unmoving as horses thudded past and the drumming of their hoofs faded away.

He forced himself upright. He had to get away, and quickly. He felt shaken but no bones seemed broken; he could move without pain. The sky was clearing and starlight revealed his Bible in the grass; he picked it up. Still shocked by the fall, he peered about, scowling as he realized he was alone. Not one man, not even Ned, had stopped to help him.

A cold fury gripped him. Someone was going to pay for that piece of treachery. He walked to his horse, then turned away; obviously that animal would never run again.

The posse couldn't be far behind and he needed a remount. Someone had been shooting at him and that someone would have a horse. He began to walk uphill, carrying his Bible.

* * *

Jo McQueen had never felt so helpless. Big Robbie, who'd seemed as permanent as any rock and someone she could rely on always to be there to back her play, lay like a log on the ground, unconscious. She ripped open his shirt to look for a bullet hole. She felt alone in the world, and desperate. Was he dead? Would he live? He had to live, had to . . . somehow this was now the most important thing in the world.

A massive shadow loomed up beside her and she turned to look up, hoping for help, but it was only the big black stallion whose stabling Robbie had shared. Nemesis had apparently come to see what was wrong. The horse's wet muzzle touched Robbie, sniffing, trying to move him.

'You and me, both,' she said in misery, fighting back tears.

A voice out of the past murmured, 'I'll just take the horse.'

She looked up. The Preacher stood there, smiling and hatless, his red hair visible in the starlight, holding a Bible. His smile faded as he looked at her, and then Robbie. He was puzzled.

'The big deputy . . . and I seem to recognize . . . no, it can't be . . . yet this looks like Fletch's horse . . . '

McQueen's voice came out so flat

she didn't recognize it as hers. 'Fletch is dead. Solo too.'

He stared at her, startled, memory stirred. '*You're* McQueen . . . ?'

He cursed Fletch viciously and opened his Bible. He brought out a revolver and aimed it at her, finger around the trigger.

'A little late, but I'll make sure this time.'

McQueen's rifle was empty, and she reached for the knife at her belt. He might kill her, but she would kill him too and Robbie would be safe.

Preacher never had the chance to shoot.

Nemesis snorted and charged. Taken by surprise, the Preacher was knocked flying, the gun leaving his hand. He fell on his back, helpless as the huge stallion reared above him.

Iron-shod hoofs smashed down, sinking into soft flesh and cracking bone beneath. Preacher screamed and tried to roll away, every movement agony.

The eyes of Nemesis glinted in the starlight and his teeth were bared ferociously as he trampled his enemy. He butted and bit, mane flying, tail lashing. He tried to lift the man's body in his mouth to shake it.

Preacher's dreadful screams became one long moaning noise. McQueen wondered if she could call Nemesis off, but doubted the stallion would obey. The black horse was in a killing rage.

His forefeet were still crashing down like hammers on an anvil. The Preacher's rib cage caved in under pounding hoofs and his moaning faded to a whimpering and then silence.

McQueen seemed to have stopped breathing. Now she took a long breath. The body was no more than a bloody pulp, the face a ruin as red as his hair when Nemesis shook himself and walked away. She shuddered. It was finally over, the Preacher dead and, again, she felt no satisfaction. Now she could . . . *what*?

She was giving her attention to

Robbie again when horses came galloping towards her. She saw Lew and Vince and a third man with a carpetbag.

Lew seemed relieved to find her in one piece. 'What the hell happened here? We could hear screaming the other side of the hill.'

She realized the third man must be the doctor from Crow Junction when he looked at the crushed body and said, 'Can't do a thing except bury this one.'

'It's the Preacher,' Jo said.

'Good riddance then.'

'My bounty!' Vince exclaimed.

The doctor crouched beside Robbie and she asked, urgently, 'Is he dead? Will he live, Doc?'

'Hmm, heart's going strong. Pulse is sound. Can't find . . . help me turn him over, Marshal.'

It took the four of them to shift Robbie's weight.

'Ah, I see it. A lump on the back of the head, a smear of blood. Nothing serious. Looks like he stepped back and fell and hit his head on a stone — knocked himself out.'

The doctor straightened up and looked at her. 'Should you feel like a bit of nursing, wash the blood away. By then he should have recovered.'

Lew said, 'See yuh later, Jo. I've got to get after the rest of the gang.' He rode off with Vince while the doctor went looking for fresh patients.

* * *

Starlight was bright on the abandoned fort on the hilltop. Inside, sheltered from the night chill, Glenn's bulldog face creased in a satisfied smile.

He was counting gold coins into canvas sacks and tying off the necks. As he worked, he hummed a tune he recalled from the past; on-stage in a melodrama, a miser counted his hoard. It was an image that had stayed with him and here he was doing that very thing.

True, it wasn't his hoard, but he still

enjoyed the counting. His audience wasn't as enthusiastic.

Sergeant Harrison had located a whiskey barrel and sprawled at ease, swallowing from a tin mug grasped in a shaky hand.

Glenn said, 'Reckon I've got most of the loot back.'

'So what?' asked the sergeant, revelling in his superior wisdom. 'You can't drink gold, fellar.'

* * *

By the time McQueen had struggled back with a hatful of water her legs ached, she was out of breath and her temper frayed. Nursemaid to a man who knocked himself out was not how she saw herself.

She found Robbie sitting up and rubbing the back of his head. 'What happened?' he asked. 'Where did you go?'

'You got a bang on the head is what happened,' she said, exasperated. 'I

239

went to get some water. You frightened the life out of me for nothing at all. Now keep still while I wash the blood away.'

'That hurts,' he complained.

'Good!'

Presently he asked, 'Where is everybody? It's gone awful quiet.'

'You remember the train robbers coming down the hill?'

His face brightened. 'Sure, I remember real good.'

'Well, they rode on by and the posse's gone after them. We're all alone, Robbie. In the moonlight.' She looked carefully at him. 'You do realize I'm a woman?'

In the almost dark, it seemed to her he wore a secret smile. 'Of course, Jo.'

'Well, you don't have to be afraid of me. I'm not going to laugh at you.'

She was beginning to get a maternal feeling about him. Well, a maternal feeling, but not exactly about him. Her feeling about him was quite a bit different. Certainly he needed help and

240

helping someone could be satisfying. He might be good for her too.

Revenge had kept her going for a while but, finally, failed her. There was no satisfaction in that.

She allowed herself to lean against him and felt a muscular arm go around her, gentle as the kiss of a feather, and didn't panic. She smiled in the twilight; it seemed her nightmare was over . . .

⋆ ⋆ ⋆

When Lew came by in the early hours, the moon was bright and Jo and Robbie were asleep in each other's arms. Like babes in the wood, he thought, but no longer innocent. Nearby, Nemesis raised a black head to stare at him before continuing to graze peacefully.

Lew looked at Jo for a long moment and reflected that, relaxed in sleep, she appeared almost beautiful.

'Looks like I'm going to have to fork

out for a wedding present,' he murmured, and measured Robbie with his eye. He rode on without disturbing them. 'Reckon it had better be a made-to-measure double bed!'

THE END